THE TRAP

THE TRAP

A NOVEL

by

TORD HUBERT

translated by
Ingrid Selberg

David McKay Company, Inc.
Ives Washburn, Inc.
New York

Originally published in Swedish by
Albert Bonniers Forlag AB, Stockholm,
under the title *Fallan*

Copyright © 1974 by Tord Hubert
English translation © Victor Gollancz Ltd 1976

All rights reserved, including the right to reproduce
this book, or parts thereof, in any form, except for
the inclusion of brief quotations in a review.

First American Edition 1977

Library of Congress Catalog Card Number 76-52556
ISBN 0-679-50755-8

10 9 8 7 6 5 4 3 2 1

MANUFACTURED IN THE UNITED STATES OF AMERICA

1

It was raining in Istanbul. Heavy clouds swept in from Asia, hung low over the pointed minarets, and emptied their contents over palaces and mosques, over the traffic jam on the Galata Bridge, and over all the employees, office girls and shop clerks who, having finished work for the day, now hurried towards the quays, where steamships lay waiting to ferry them across to the other side of the Bosporus.

He enjoyed sitting on the inside of a rain-streaked window, observing the afflicted world outside. It gave him the same feeling as sitting in a comfortable armchair and watching people destroy each other on television. A feeling of security. Misleading certainly, but pleasant nonetheless.

He ordered a beer. The Liman Restaurant overlooked the Bosporus on the north side of the entrance to the Golden Horn, the inlet which divides Istanbul into two parts. Out in the strait two Russian destroyers with covered gun muzzles headed towards the Black Sea, hammer and sickle drooping astern. A large Crisscraft speedboat crossed their wake. Its radarscope and radio aerial identified it as a NATO patrol boat.

An ice-cold Tuborg arrived and he drank it slowly while watching the destroyers. This strait, where Europe and Asia meet, had always been the setting for dramatic political confrontations. It was one of the most blood-stained spots in the world. Over the centuries people had sacrificed their lives here for the belief in their own cultural superiority; Greeks and Persians, Christians and Moslems. Now it was East and West that took their turn.

He smiled to himself. By and large, there was only one culture which was readily accepted the world over—the Danish beer-culture. Wherever you travelled, you could count on quenching your thirst with a bottle of Tuborg.

'Mr Martin, I presume.'

The man addressing him was in his fifties. He stood at the edge of the table and made a vague gesture towards a copy of *Time* which lay next to a vase of dark red roses. From his inner pocket he drew out an identical issue of *Time* and placed it next to the one already on the table.

'My name is Dr Goretz. MEET ME IN ISTANBUL LIMAN RESTAURANT FIRST MONDAY IN JUNE AT 18.30. IDENTIFY WITH TIME NUMBER 22. I know your message by heart. I'm pleased to meet you, Mr Martin. May I sit down? Now, what shall we eat?'

He sat down and reached out for a menu.

Dr Goretz spoke English with an accent like a German professor in a wartime spy film. He also looked the part with his thick grey hair, gold-rimmed glasses and baggy suit. But Martin never judged anyone by appearances—least of all Dr Goretz. His hair looked too thick at the temples and the parting seemed to have a false bottom. He was wearing a hairpiece. The glasses were probably part of the same disguise. And perhaps the suit fitted so poorly because it was not his own.

'Grape leaf *dolmades*,' suggested Dr Goretz, 'aubergine salad, prawns, crab salad, olives, goat cheese and a few tomatoes. Why not some *pastirma*, which is a type of dried lamb? And of course, we will drink *raki*, an arrack spirit, much like French *pernod* or *pastis* or Greek *ouzo*. After a few glasses you can eat anything. *Raki* is the prerequisite for all Turkish meals!'

'I'll have beer.'

Dr Goretz ordered the meal and the waiter disappeared across the vast floor. The Liman Restaurant was not like most modern restaurants, which calculate their profitability per square centimetre of customer. On the contrary, it had a very high ceiling and the tables were so far apart that they seemed like islands in a sea of parquet. Which made it perfect for undisturbed conversations.

'Your first visit to Istanbul, Mr Martin?'

'No.'

'A remarkable place, don't you think? Do you see the palace with the green copper roof on the other side of the Horn? That's the Seraglio, as I'm sure you know, Mr Martin. Perhaps you've also heard of Sultan Ibrahim? One day when he tired of the thousands of women in his harem, he had them stuffed into sacks and drowned. Right out there.' He pointed to the water below the Seraglio. 'Then he picked himself a brand new harem. They say Istanbul hasn't changed much since then.'

'Which brings us to the subject of our business.'

'Quite right, Mr Martin. The goods are ready for delivery according to your wishes. Place Malmö. And payment?'

'Here.' Martin drew a visiting card out from his coat pocket and put it on the table in front of Dr Goretz. 'Help yourself.'

Dr Goretz picked up the card, which read: ROBERT MARTIN. EXPORT-IMPORT. LEIDSEKADE 25 AMSTERDAM.

'I don't understand,' he said. The agreed payment was a quarter of a million German marks, and you're giving me your card?'

'Hold it up to the light.'

Dr Goretz lifted the card up towards the window. Eight small rectangles were outlined like shadows in the paper.

'Stamps!' he exclaimed. 'Perfect. It couldn't be more discreet. Or safer, so I have heard. You can carry your fortune in your pocket wherever you travel. No need to worry about currency regulations or customs. And who would ever suspect that a few visiting cards contain stamps worth millions?'

'If you'd like to convert the stamps into ready cash, I recommend Robson Lowe in Basel; they'll give you a fair deal. However, I suggest that you hold on to them as long as possible. The rate of increase in the value of stamps is much higher than bank interest or stock dividends. You can count on at least twenty per cent a year.'

'If we weren't in desperate need of capital, we'd never make a deal like this.'

'In that case I must ask you to remove the stamps from the card before you go to the stamp dealer. Soak the card in lukewarm water. Let the glue dissolve. The stamps will loosen and float to the surface. Then dry them in a press. But do be careful. Even the slightest damage means a loss of thousands of marks in their value. As a matter of fact, a perforation on a rare stamp is the world's most valuable object in proportion to its size.'

The waiter returned with a tray covered with bowls of *hors d'oeuvres* which he set out on the table. The conversation stopped. Dr Goretz stuck the visiting card into his wallet. The rain beat on the window pane. Out on the Bosporus the Russian destroyers had long since disappeared from view. It was slowly growing dark.

'I'm pleased that our price was accepted without objections,' said Dr Goretz. 'A quarter of a million German marks is a lot of money. But then people are a rare commodity today. Unlike in Sultan Ibrahim's time, they're not for sale. At least not for complete consumption. No return, so to speak.'

He helped himself to another *dolmades*, cut it in half and stuffed one piece into his mouth. Opening his eyes wide, he smacked his lips noisily.

'Delicious.'

'My employer hasn't complained about the price,' said Martin. 'Did you make enquiries of the other side?'

'If you mean with your colleagues in Syria and Lebanon, then the answer is no. They do train the same sort of specialists as you do, and they're also willing to sell them if the price is right. For complete consumption, as you called it. But they can't fulfil the language requirement.'

'Both of ours speak Swedish—one of them very well. But they do have accents, and therefore usually pass for Danes when working in Sweden and vice versa.'

'Yes. I'm ready to hear their particulars now.'

'Will you take notes?' Dr Goretz refilled his plate from the bowls.

'In my profession there's only one reliable place for notes. In one's mind.'

'Do help yourself, Mr Martin. The *dolmades* are exquisite. And try the crab salad.' He pushed a few of the bowls closer to Martin. 'The first name is Mladen Steiner. Age twenty-seven. Training: two years at our school in Spain, one in Portugal. Speciality: the Swedish language. The second name: Milan Moll. Age forty-two. Training: two years at our school in Argentina and a year in Portugal. Speciality: explosives. During the year in Portugal Steiner and Moll trained together extensively. Assignment: to promote our cause among Yugoslavians abroad. Area of operation: Sweden.'

'Do you have any special reason for letting us have them?'

'Our tactics are changing. More and more we're restricting our activities to our own country. We feel propaganda is a better weapon than terror. Hitler's big mistake with the Jews was that he concentrated on eradication. And what was the result? The same as when you try to exterminate vermin with DDT. The strain develops a resistance. That's why we concentrate on persuasion and information. But, as I'm sure you know, Mr Martin, psychological influences are much more demanding and costly than physical ones. In other words, we need money—not terrorists like Steiner and Moll.'

As he spoke, Dr Goretz played with the glass of *raki* in his hands. His hands were soft and sensitive. A humanitarian's hands. Unsuitable for plunging a knife into someone, but designed to write death sentences by the hundreds.

'Has their work been satisfactory?' asked Martin.

'You paid for first-class material, Mr Martin, and first-class material is what you'll get. Steiner and Moll have been working in Sweden since 1967. In Denmark as well. Completely satisfactory. Their anonymity remains unbroken. They were neither involved in the murder of Ambassador Rolovic, nor in the hijacking of the SAS jet between Gothenburg and Stockholm and the subsequent release of our imprisoned comrades. The police don't know they exist.'

'I notice you didn't mention the sabotage of the Yugoslav Airline's DC-9 in January 1972. I seem to remember that it took off in Stockholm, stopped over in Copenhagen, and exploded in the air over Czechoslovakia.'

Dr Goretz smiled.

'I can assure you, Mr Martin, that the fact that the hostess Miss Vukovic survived did not depend on the inefficiency of Steiner and Moll, but on incredible luck. I can also guarantee you that the Swedish police found no trace of who planted the bomb in the hold of the jet at Ärlanda airport in Stockholm.'

Martin nodded and the two concentrated on eating. They were two distinctly different types of eaters. Dr Goretz ate with rapture as if he were taking Communion, while Martin filled himself dutifully.

'Do we agree on the details of the transfer?' asked Martin.

'Yes. We suggest the seventeenth of next month. Steiner and Moll will get their orders on the evening of the sixteenth. The next day they'll be on location. Address: Föreningsgatan 19, Malmö.'

Dr Goretz paused to let Martin take in the address.

'You do have a peculiar profession, Mr Martin.'

'I doubt whether you know much about my profession, Dr Goretz.'

'In that case, I don't think you know much about mine. I deal in information. Naturally I've collected information on you as well.'

Dr Goretz wiped his mouth with a napkin and set it aside on the table. 'You're a businessman,' he continued. 'But not just an ordinary businessman. You deal in goods, but not just ordinary goods. Only unobtainable goods. If someone in Ireland needs weapons to shoot with, then Mr Martin always knows someone in Prague who can supply machine guns. Or if certain importers in Milan feel that the duty on cigarettes is too high, they can turn to Mr Martin with confidence. He can easily obtain some West German customs seals. A transport lorry sealed with West German seals takes care of all customs problems.'

'Not easily,' Martin smiled. 'The seals cost me twenty thousand marks.'

'The profit on the fact that a transport lorry loaded with cigarettes passes unexamined and untaxed at the border must have been about half a million. Twenty thousand for seals is a trifling sum. Anyway, I assume you sold them afterwards for five times their original price.'

'Speaking of money, Dr Goretz, let me take care of the bill. I was here first.'

Martin beckoned the waiter and paid. They took the lift down to the street, where the stench of petrol, garlic and the rotting old town engulfed them. Although the rain had stopped, the streets were still wet. They hailed a taxi and went to a nightclub on a side street off Istiklal Caddesi, near Taksim Square.

A bowing head waiter welcomed and seated them in one of the booths with a good view of the stage. Martin waved away the hostesses who drifted up to the table. He ordered whisky without ice or water. Dr Goretz continued drinking *raki*. There were some couples on the dance floor. Most of the tables were occupied. The guests were exclusively men.

'Have you ever been to Zagreb, Mr Martin?'

Martin shook his head.

'Perhaps you'll go there someday. If you do, stay at the Esplanade, one of Europe's most elegant hotels. Marble, brass, velvet. What a nightclub! And what women!'

'Just wait until the floorshow begins. This place is also renowned for its women. They combine European elegance with Asiatic abandon, refinement with decadence.'

'Zagreb!' Dr Goretz refilled his glass. 'One evening go to Trg Republice, the heart and soul of Croatia. Listen to the newsboys crying *Vjesnik* and *Sport*, and to the streetcars clattering out from Ilica Avenue and rumbling towards the crowd at the market. Go into a café in Neboder and get to know some Croats. Admire their proud bearing and their beautiful women. Those are our people. One day we'll be back with them again. One day Croatia will be freed. Here's to Croatia! And here's to your employer, Mr Martin. I gather you're fighting for freedom also.'

'Everyone is.'

Martin had been dismayed by Dr Goretz's nationalist outburst, but now he realized what Goretz was after. Information. He was using the intimacy trick: if I confide in you, then you'll confide in me.

'Perhaps everyone is,' answered Dr Goretz, 'but not everyone can afford to spend a quarter of a million German marks.'

'Dear Doctor, I assure you, I have no clue to my employer's identity. I received my orders from a messenger. I report back to a poste restante address. Those are my working conditions. I'm the necessary link between buyers and sellers in a market where both parties must remain anonymous.'

'Yes, yes,' said Goretz. 'Of course. Sometimes my curiosity runs away with me. An occupational side-effect, I think.'

The show began with a fanfare from the orchestra. During the next hour one girl after another flaunted her physical assets in well-rehearsed numbers. Some undressed in traditional striptease style, others undulated in Oriental dances, shedding scarf after scarf.

When the show was finished, the girls paraded around the club, listening to offers and selling themselves to the highest bidders.

Martin set his eye on a twenty-five-year-old Persian girl with long, coal-black hair, slender limbs and large breasts.

'What's the highest offer you've had so far?' he asked, when she reached his table.

'One hundred and fifty dollars.'

'Then I'll offer one hundred and twenty-five,' he replied, thereby showing that although he could not be tricked, he was still generous.

2

She couldn't find a parking space in Strandvägen, but an illegally parked car would serve her purpose just as well. She pulled in behind it, took the yellow traffic ticket out from under the windscreen wipers, and placed it on her own Fiat instead. In Stockholm's traffic jungle no journalist could get by without one trick or another, although she felt that the reporter who kept crutches lying in his car so that he could park in places reserved for invalids went a bit too far.

She checked her watch. Still two minutes left. She ran across the street.

In the lift she examined herself in the mirror. No lipstick, no eye make-up, just a lot of freckles on her nose which she couldn't get rid of. Wrinkles already around the corners of her eyes at twenty-five, but what could she do about it? Smile less? Go to bed earlier? She recalled something she'd once written about a famous singer: he didn't look a day over thirty, but a hell of a lot of nights! She combed her hair. It was brown and long and hung loosely over her shoulders.

When she stepped out on to the third floor, a uniformed guard stopped her.

'Identification, please.'

She produced her press card, which he snatched away. Telling her to wait, he disappeared through the double doors into a corridor where two more guards stood.

She looked around. Everything was marble, brass and mahogany —just as imposing and full of memories of a glorious past as a cemetery. She knew that the senator had the entire floor at his disposal for the week. She went over to the window. The palace lay basking in the evening sun. A light grey battleship was reflected in the sky-blue water of Alvsnabban. Sweden was a hypocritical country. At the same time as this warship voyaged round the world, advertising Sweden with its uniforms and cannons, in Stockholm the prime minister talked about the importance of eliminating all violence in the world.

'This way.'

The guard returned her press card and led her through the double doors into the hall and up to a white door with large panels and a lovely brass doorknob.

'Wait here,' said the guard, and went back the same way.

She wondered if she had reached the last door. Perhaps the senator was that sort of powerful man who liked hiding behind a series of doors in order to impress his followers with the Chinese-box effect: step by step increasing their expectations of what lay in the inner sanctum. An effective tactic, but also dangerous. One risked creating the opposite effect: an anti-climax, powerful enough to cause his downfall.

A short man appeared from one of the doors and informed her that he was responsible for the security of the senator and that his name was Maclean. He had slim hips, a powerful chest and broad shoulders, one of those men who widened at the top in a way which always reminded Anna of a genie emerging from a bottle.

He showed her into a room which was conspicuously empty, with bare white walls and a wide parquet floor without a carpet. Behind a desk by the window sat the principal figure in the room. When he rose to greet her she recognized him from the colour photos at the editorial office. He was the archetypal American senator: tall, well built, with silver in his hair and gold in his mouth, and searching blue eyes that made him look as if he were determined to seek out all honest people and give them their just rewards.

'Senator Stockwell, Miss Anna Berger,' the security chief introduced them.

'Welcome,' said the senator. 'I must say that, despite this unfortunate photograph which is the reason for our meeting.'

'It's one of the best photos I've seen,' said Anna.

Maclean switched on the projector on the desk which cast a picture on the white wall. She knew it well. It was a copy of the photo that lay at the newspaper office, awaiting publication. It showed Senator Stockwell on a walk in Humlegården park together with Konstantin Feodorov, a member of the Russian Politburo. Flowers dazzled red and yellow; a few children played on the grass. In the foreground a flock of pigeons flew up from the gravel walk in front of the men's feet.

'Caption!'

The senator picked up a letter from his desk. Anna recognized it, the chief editor had shown it to her before sending it.

'In large white letters on the left above the pigeons: THEY WILL BRING PEACE IN OUR TIME.'

'Yes,' said Anna.

The senator smiled.

'Now,' he said. 'I've often noticed that pretty girls like you have more luck than they deserve. On the other hand, that's exactly what pretty girls like you deserve. Of course, you realize that right now you're on the verge of getting a world scoop.'

Anna smiled back. But carefully. She knew that the senator had the same taste for attractive young women as so many other American leaders, a tradition as deeply rooted in American politics as that of presidential assassination. He had the same sound academic background as Henry Kissinger and expected to achieve the same importance in American foreign politics, if not greater. He had belonged to the intimate circle around Teddy Kennedy for a long time. But a year ago he had broken away, created his own image, and gone his own separate way. More and more he was becoming known as the disarmament senator. His political appearances resembled revivalist meetings, where world peace was salvation. The response was always tremendous. His personality gave people faith and hope in a better world. He had that combination of innocence and fighting spirit which characterizes all born saviours. He had great political experience as well, and was recognized as a skilful negotiator. He even spoke fluent Russian, from the time he had spent as a liaison officer in Berlin right after the war, and he had many personal friends among the Russian political leadership. Some people predicted that he might be the next president of the USA and most were sure that he would at least become vice-president, but everyone agreed that he had a great political future ahead.

'Please sit down,' the senator indicated the chairs by the desk. 'You're planning to print that picture of Feodorov, me and the doves of peace, and I can't prevent you. Therefore, I'm making a virtue out of necessity and granting you an interview. At least in this way, I'll avoid being attacked with a mass of false rumours.'

'Are you conducting private negotiations on disarmament with Feodorov?' asked Anna.

The senator nodded.

'Which specific questions are you discussing?'

'For nearly one hundred years the great powers have negotiated about disarmament. As you know, no progress has been made. We haven't even been able to check the immense re-armament. Quite the contrary. Today the arms race is greater than ever before. It costs two hundred billion a year, which is more than the combined national revenues of all the underdeveloped countries in the world. Since the disarmament negotiations began in Geneva in 1962, the number of inter-continental missiles has increased five-fold. Your compatriot, the famous Alva Myrdal, has come to the most discouraging conclusion of the year in Geneva, namely that none of the great powers have serious intentions at the disarmament negotiations. Nor does she believe that they will in the future, unless, as she says, a catharsis of such intensity occurs that it causes conversion.'

The senator ran his fingers through his silver hair and looked up at the ceiling.

'I see this as my mission. I've taken Mrs Myrdal's words upon me. I shall do my utmost to bring about a catharsis of such intensity that it causes conversion. I will arouse in people an awareness of what is at stake. Mankind is standing at a crossroads. Either it continues as before, which will lead to certain destruction before AD 2000, or it can concentrate on radical disarmament.'

The senator spoke with both authority and solemnity, Anna thought. But without the pomposity which made many other politicians sound as if they were God delivering a proclamation to mankind.

'How will you bring about this conversion?'

'I will appeal to people's sense of humanity. And to their instinct of self-preservation. I'm going to make world peace and disarmament the focus of my campaign in the next presidential election.'

'And your meeting with Feodorov here in Sweden. Are you also trying to appeal to his sense of humanity?'

'Feodorov and I have been old friends since we both served in Berlin right after the war. We had many of the same ideas already then. Since that time, we've both been working in our own parts of the world to further these ideas. Now it looks as if we might soon be able to work together openly. From our meeting here in Stockholm we've drafted a four-point programme which includes disarmament. Within half a year of my winning the presidential election, the first real disarmament agreement will be signed and sealed.'

He rose and gazed thoughtfully out of the window at the world he'd resolved to save from destruction.

Anna wondered how much of his eagerness for peace was sincere idealism, and how much was a tactical move to win the presidential election. Was he a fraud, soon to be exposed, or a sincere saviour, who maybe could make the world a better place? Or a little of both, like so many other evangelists?

She couldn't help suspecting him. On the other hand, she mistrusted her suspicions as no more than a journalist's chronic scepticism about the existence of sincere idealism in public figures. She recalled how she had once heard Olaf Palme speaking about solidarity and equality at an election rally in Halmstad and how she'd made the scornful notes on her pad: over-enthusiastic, rhetorical. Then, afterwards, they had met in the wings. There was Palme sitting on a crate, shrunken, head in hands, a victim of dismay, who transformed her from a reporter into a mother confessor. He spoke about the feelings behind his words. If there is no real feeling behind the words, then they sound false and empty, he said. When you begin as a politician, it is easy. The feelings give birth to the words, the words convince people. But then? When the words are repeated and repeated and then repeated one hundred times more? Certainly the feeling is still there, but it no longer has the intensity to give life to the words. You need to boost them with a little artifice. Palme was unhappy. He felt like a bad actor. What did it matter that he was a great idealist?

Maybe Stockwell was in the same boat as Palme. Anyway, who was she to judge between false and sincere idealism? Did it in fact matter whether Stockwell's idealism was sincere? Perhaps false idealism achieved its goals more easily. As McLuhan noticed, if our actions are repeated frequently they eventually become our nature.

The senator turned towards her.

'The unique factor in the proposal discussed between Feodorov and myself is that we link the disarmament question with the issue of aid to developing countries. The arms race is a mindless waste of resources. The UN report on disarmament and its development since 1972 reveals some interesting figures: each year the world spends about sixty billion dollars on research and science. Of this, about twenty-five billion goes to military research. Imagine what fantastic results could be achieved if this sum were spent on constructive development instead! Let me give you an example. When nuclear disarmament becomes a fact, more than twenty thousand scientists and highly qualified technicians will be redundant. They could be rechannelled to work on atomic energy for peaceful purposes in developing countries. What a tremendous step forward!'

'What are the four points of your disarmament proposal?'

'I can't reveal that until the time is ripe. The results of our negotiations are still a joint secret.'

'Even your meeting took place in greatest secrecy. If this photo of you and Feodorov hadn't been taken, no one would have known that you'd even met in Stockholm. May I ask why all this secrecy?'

'For security reasons.'

'When I came I noticed that the security precautions here are rigorous. Armed guards, identification check, and so forth. Do you feel your life is in danger?'

'No, but without these precautions, I would.' He smiled again and motioned towards the security chief. 'Maclean can explain.'

'Yes,' said the security chief. 'I can. On several occasions there have been assassination attempts against the senator. Three letter bombs were addressed to him, twice snipers have shot at him, and an explosive charge was discovered in his car and dismantled. All this within the last thirty days.'

'Here in Stockholm as well?'

'One of the letter bombs arrived at this address, yes.'

'Do you know who's after your life?' She turned towards the senator.

He shrugged his shoulders.

'A man in my position must count on having enemies. In addition, if disarmament is the major point in his political platform then he must count on deadly enemies. Both in the East and the West. The advocates of the arms industry are powerful. And ruthless. I really don't want to say any more. But I'll remind you of the Watergate scandal. The essential issue at stake was not that Nixon tampered with the tapes. It was that America's own security police spied on the Democratic party's presidential candidate, Senator McGovern, well known for his involvement in the peace movement.'

He looked at his watch.

'I'm sorry,' he said. 'But I do have so many commitments.'

Anna rose.

'What are your plans for the near future? When are you leaving Sweden?'

'I'll be staying on a few days. Feodorov has already returned to Moscow. I'm going to relax for the first time in months. No conferences, no interviews, no telephone calls. For once, I'm going to indulge myself in my hobby.'

'What's that?'

'I think the senator would prefer his hobby to remain private,' interrupted the security chief.

'You make it sound as if I'm chasing girls,' laughed the senator. He turned to Anna. 'Actually I'm going to pursue some far more cold-blooded creatures.'

'Senator, that's enough now.'

'He behaves more and more as if we were married!' The

senator took Anna's hand. 'An old-fashioned marriage. I'm the downtrodden housewife. Take my advice: never marry.'

In the lift she combed her hair again and then felt ready to face the crowds strolling along Strandvägen. It was a lovely summer evening, and there were swarms of people taking the last opportunity to build up their resistance before the hard winter came to plunder yet another year of their lives.

She crossed the street and removed the parking ticket from the window of her Fiat, but couldn't return it to its rightful owner, who'd driven away. She got in and drove off.

Outside the newspaper office in Torsgatan there were always plenty of parking places after five o'clock. She parked the Fiat close to the entrance and took the lift. Her department was the only one still at work. Another two hours until the deadline. On evenings when the magazine was going to press the office sounded like a classroom when the teacher has just left the room. Telephones rang, typewriters clattered, raised voices debated the crucial question of how much one could show of the princess's breast.

'Oh, there you are at last,' said the chief editor. 'Did you get hold of the peace apostle? Good. There'll only be half the space for your copy. Do it in two columns, twenty lines long and fifty-seven letters across. We'll lay the photo on a double-page spread. Jesus! Flowers, children, pigeons and two secret peace negotiators all in one go. Do you know what we'll use for the caption?'

'They will bring peace in our time.'

'That's right. Then underneath something about a better world, and that history is being made in Humlegården park. Then your copy. Did he say anything?'

'Yes. He promised to have the first of four points in his disarmament proposal accomplished within half a year of the presidential election. If he wins, that is. Also, that there've been many assassination attempts. He got a letter bomb at his address on Strandvägen. Snipers are after him, an explosive charge was found in his car and so on.'

'Great! We'll use that. Murder and assassination are far more sensational than peace and a better world. We'll change the caption underneath to: They strove for peace but their lives are in danger. Jesus, this is a major world issue. What incredible luck Ken had to be sitting on that bench in Humlegården park and see them coming.'

'Yes.'

'Luck, who knows... I wonder if his luck wasn't given a boost by the senator's PR men. This photo will be printed all over the world. It'll be shown on TV everywhere. Including the USA. Secret peace negotiations are all right, but the secret has to leak out somehow to have any PR value. This is the perfect way to do it: attractive colour photos, intriguing hints, a little information dropped here, a little there. A puzzle where half the pieces consist of the public's own fantasies. I wonder if Ken didn't get a tip-off about those men in Humlegården park. After all, he's an American too. In fact, isn't he involved in the peace movement?'

'He's a deserter, or was at one time. It's ages ago now. But I'll ask him. We'll be meeting tonight.'

'Oh yes, that's right. You're both going to the mountains together. Our girl in the wilderness. I can see you now: mosquitoes, blackflies, cold rain, wind, wet feet, scraggly hair. You've got a delightful week ahead of you.'

The telephone rang.

'I thought it'd gone dead,' he said, 'I haven't been interrupted for nearly three minutes now.'

He picked up the receiver and Anna went to her own office. She wasn't disappointed that the space for her copy had been cut by half. That was part of her job. In a matter of minutes a four-page article could be slashed down to four lines. All for the sake of the whole paper. This sacred whole consisted of the editorial management's occasional whims, personal foibles and confused speculations about what the readership wanted, which was always the same: sex, sport, and the opportunity to be outraged by a social issue.

She sat down at her typewriter. Two columns. She would only have room for a short introduction about the senator and a shortened version of the interview. All that research was unnecessary. She stuffed the cuttings lying on the table back into their green folder. Two columns containing facts, only facts.

There'd be about as much room for her personal interpretation as in a recipe for meatballs.

She started with five lines on world peace and disarmament, continued with ten lines about the assassination attempts, then quoted fifteen lines from the interview, rounded off by a look at the senator's career, and ended by predicting that he would be the next president of the USA.

She looked at the clock. Half an hour to go before the deadline. She lingered on in her office and enjoyed the silence. The department she'd worked in previously had been a gigantic open-plan area. There had been no door to close so she had closed herself in. She had withdrawn completely instead of letting her personality flow freely as it must for a journalist.

Being a magazine journalist involved going out into the world, gathering bits of real life, taking them home to the deepest cellar of her mind to be flavoured by the other experiences stored there. She could have written this article about the senator just as well in the office.

She went into the main editorial department where the princess's breast was just going to press; proof that respect for individual privacy was always the first victim in the battle for increased circulation. She put her typed copy on the chief editor's desk. His eyes scanned it quickly, then he nodded and said thanks and goodbye.

She took the lift down, started up the Fiat, drove along Torsgatan, crossed St Eriksplan and stopped outside Svensson and Butler. He stood outside waiting. She recognized him by the soft camera bag which all professional photographers carried around now, ever since the square leather cases had gone out of fashion. Although she did not know him, she had heard a lot about him. He had a reputation for never leaving alone any girl who was within his arms' reach. She did not want to become his newest triumph.

She locked the car and walked over to him. He looked as if he had stepped out of a magazine illustration: his height, broad shoulders, unruly blond hair, brown eyes, strong jaw. His handshake was a little more literary, like that of a sales representative for books, a warm firm grip which lasted just long enough to make her aware of the bodily contact without feeling threatened.

'Nice to meet you,' he said.

They walked through the shop's jumble of lovely and unnecessary gifts and sat down opposite each other at one of the long tables with chequered tablecloths. A few seats away at the same table sat two elderly ladies, wearing white hats, with a bottle of red wine between them. A gang of young people occupied most of the other long tables. No more guests were needed to make the place crowded.

'Your photo of Senator Stockwell is fantastic,' said Anna. 'How did you take it? Were you tipped off?'

'No, it was pure luck. I was just sitting on a bench, sunning myself. Then they came walking by, and I said to myself, isn't that old Stockwell over there? So I snapped away a few times, and when the pigeons took flight it couldn't have been better if I'd planned it. They didn't even notice they were being photographed.'

Anna was surprised that she couldn't detect the slightest accent in Ken. Obviously he had shed his past. He hadn't buried himself like so many other deserters, but had been eager to adapt himself to Swedish life. After a photography course he'd worked for the *Express* and made his career free-lancing, first as a fashion and pin-up photographer and then as a general news photographer.

'We'll be camping together this week,' he said. 'It should be fun. A great break. A perfect publicity stunt for a new tourist scheme. Experience the authentic wilderness life with all the modern conveniences!'

'It sounds awful.'

'I'm sure it isn't. Tourist personnel are very capable nowadays. This scheme is a fisherman's paradise, especially tailored for Deutschmark tourists. If we can't use our wilderness, then we sell it to the Germans.'

The waitress came and Ken ordered Tuborgs for them both, sautéed kidneys for Anna and an entrecôte for himself.

'There are many angles to this,' he said. 'Europe is splitting into two parts, an industrial Europe and a leisure-time Europe. The boundary will be drawn just north of Malmö, with Stockholm as an island in the recreation paradise.'

'Yes, but it's too bad about the European industrial workers, don't you think? During the day they work as parts of the machines they operate; at night they're stacked on top of each other in blocks of flats. They could well use coming here for a week, breathing fresh air and feeling like people.'

'You don't know what you're talking about. Gone are the days when a poor worker could look forward to fresh air and clean water in the open country. Now it's only a privilege for the rich. Surely you don't imagine it'll be cheap to fly up to Norrland from Hamburg to fish for a week!'

'That's true,' said Anna.

'But for those who can afford it, it'll be fantastic. Just a few hours after leaving Germany, they'll land in a stretch of wilderness which really deserves to be called the wide open spaces. In addition there's a river which God has obligingly stocked with an excess of salmon trout. With the Tourist Board's help, of course.'

The food came, and Anna discovered that she enjoyed Ken's company within the safe walls of the surrounding noise. They talked about their imminent trip, about packing, and what time Ken should come to collect her in the morning. Conversation darted back and forth between them, freely and easily, like swallows on a summer evening.

She let her glance linger on his face and strong hands and thought that if she hadn't made it a matter of principle never to powder her freckles, then this would have been an occasion when she would at least have toned them down a little.

But when they said goodnight at her Fiat he made a few lovely compliments about her freckles and even more about the rest of her appearance. He squeezed her hand twice as hard as when they had met, but still didn't make her feel threatened. It was only in the car on the way home that she remembered once writing that flattery was no more than describing a woman's appearance in terms sufficiently exaggerated to agree with her own opinion of herself.

3

THE SAS DC-9 from Stockholm touched down softly with its front tyre on the rain-wet concrete, landed safely on all three and curtseyed prettily over the front tyre while braking. Slowly the plane taxied towards the airport buildings.

The major stood inside the glass doors, breathing the smell of brewing coffee which characterized Norrland as the smell of garlic does southern Italy. He didn't feel eager to go through the same welcoming procedure for the third time. That morning he'd met two guests from Denmark at the railway station, and, at noon, two from Stockholm at Kiruna Airport. This was not exactly the life he had foreseen, when he'd left the army half a year ago. He already missed the safe grey cocoon of his uniform. His new butterfly existence, as the PR director of the Tourist Association, did not suit him. The nectar was pleasing, the salary doubled, but he detested the fluttering: dinners, the calls, entertainment, speeches and handshaking. Not to speak of the necessity for courtesy. In the army he'd only had to salute superiors. Now he had to be friendly to everyone, in the same way as a car dealer.

The plane had stopped, and the passengers streamed down the steps and hurried through the drizzle towards the shelter of the buildings. The major easily identified his guests. Doctor Haseke was a grey-bearded man, a bit beyond his forties like the major, but taller and stronger. He wore a startling hat with a gaudy collection of fishing flies around its brim, and was accompanied by an equally startling secretary. The major followed her with his eyes as she proceeded over the field next to the doctor. She was blonde and was dressed completely in brown. The short lumberjacket was dark brown, her jumper and tight-fitting trousers were light brown, the gloves and leather boots were rust brown. She looked as if her only previous contact with nature had been the plastic branches with which German boutiques love to decorate their autumn window displays.

'Doktor Haseke, verstehe ich,' said the major, when the German came through the glass doors with his secretary. 'Ich bin Major Nilsson. Villkommen, Herr Doktor.'

'Thanks,' said the German. 'But let's speak in Swedish. Don't be surprised. My organization feels that their Scandinavian director should speak at least one of the Nordic languages. Let me introduce my secretary, Fräulein Krämer.'

She offered the major a soft, feminine hand with long, dark red nails and a little smile of the same colour. The skilfully dishevelled hair framed a soft face, where nothing disrupted the impression of a perfect façade—no wrinkles, no scars or other irregularities such as character or personality.

'I do apologize for the weather,' the major said to the doctor. 'I'd hoped to welcome you with warmth and sunshine.'

'If I'm not mistaken,' said the doctor, 'there were glaciers here as recently as eight thousand years ago. It's not surprising that the climate can be a bit harsh even today.'

'That's right. Harsh, but healthy. They say there's no such thing as bad weather, except in cities.'

'Isn't Kiruna the world's largest town?'

'Yes, but what I mean are rather the large industrial...'

'A joke, Major,' interrupted the doctor.

'I see. Anyway, our destination lies outside the boundaries of Kiruna.'

The baggage arrived on two carts, and the major helped his guests lift down their bags. He hailed a taxi driver and let him carry everything to the car while he spoke.

'I'm sorry,' he said. 'Normally you'd have gone straight from the plane to the helicopter. Unfortunately the helicopter I'd hired for today had a motor breakdown, so we'll have to fly by hydroplane. It only takes twenty minutes to get to the plane by taxi.'

They sped through the flat landscape towards Kiruna, which spread out on the south side of a low mountain, between the two ore-bearing mountains Kirunavaara and Luossavaara, which because of their step-like terraces looked rather as if they were being built up instead of torn down. When he neared Kiruna, the major always felt as if he had reached the farthest outpost of civilization, a feeling which combined both admiration for those people who lived there and relief because he himself did not. At the foot of Mount Kiruna they turned left and drove away from the city towards Nikkaluokta and Kebnekaise. Doctor

Haseke announced that he planned to stop over in Kiruna for a few days on the journey home, and they chatted for a while about what was worth seeing there. Then they arrived at Rakkurijärvi, where a white Cessna 206 with red mountain markings on the tail and wings lay by the landing dock, waiting for them.

The major spotted Peter Baxter, who emerged from the airline's office and came over to meet them. He wore faded jeans, a worn army jacket and dusty wellingtons, and looked as if he had just come out of the wilderness and couldn't wait to return there.

He introduced Peter to the others. Peter was accompanying them up to the mountains. He was English and had been teaching at the Hjalmar Lundboms School in Kiruna for three years, but his only real interests were wildlife and salmon fishing. He hoped to work as a warden at a fishing lodge the following summer.

Then the pilot came out of the office, chatted and shook hands, and stowed the bags in the plane. He helped them into the blue interior and placed the Germans opposite the Englishman and the major.

'We're off now,' he said over the intercom. He started up the engine, and taxied out from the landing stage towards the north side of the water for a take-off position against the wind. He accelerated in order to test the magnetos at 2,000 revolutions, pulled in the control stick to the water rudder, folded out the wing flaps and called to the control tower.

'Philip Rudolf, Philip Rudolf, requesting a take-off position.' Then he accelerated again and the plane shot off across the water surface, until the pontoons lifted and the plane mounted towards the grey skies in the south-west. Seven or eight minutes later they left Kiruna's controlled area at a height of five hundred metres and a cruising speed of 240 kilometres per hour. Below them the northern landscape spread out with its birches, lakes, marshes and fields. It rose before them uninterrupted, the foot-hills growing higher and higher, but poor visibility prevented them from seeing the high mountains.

'Is an aeroplane really the only means of approach?' asked Doctor Haseke.

'Yes, that's what's unique about our scheme,' said the major. 'We place our guests in the wilderness at least one hundred kilometres away from the nearest settlement, far away from fences, telephones and television. That's why we're calling the scheme Operation Wilderness. Where the harassed city-dweller can relax and live a real pioneer life under completely safe conditions, of course, and with all modern conveniences.'

'It sounds exotic. For German fishing enthusiasts it'll sound just as exciting as Srinagar in Kashmir. And yet it fits perfectly into the ordinary package holiday schemes. Emphasize the special attraction such as swimming, skiing or, in this case, fishing and let the rest be as much like the traveller's own home as possible: food, beds, social life. We can fill up a Caravelle bound for Kiruna each week with no problems. The question is whether you can cope with the entire load.'

'When the scheme is completed by next summer, we'll have ten cabins with room for fifteen persons in each. All first class.'

'If the charter plane is filled to capacity, then air travel is just as cheap today as the pneumatic dispatch was years ago. Just as impersonal too, but that doesn't matter if it's quick.'

The major could just about follow the German travel tycoon's calculations. He knew that they could make a clear profit of five hundred marks per person if everything went as planned, which would mean an income of about a million marks during the ten weeks the season lasted. If everything went as planned, that is.

'Guck Hansi,' said Fräulein Krämer, and pointed out through the window. 'Was ist das?' She'd sighted a huge reindeer enclosure underneath them. It looked like a child's drawing of a sunflower with a gigantic pistil in the centre and about ten small semi-circular petals around it.

The major explained in his best German. He told her how the Lapps herded the reindeer into the big enclosure in the centre, and then each owner caught his own reindeer with a lasso, drew them into the smaller pens around the side, and there marked or slaughtered them, depending on the season.

A quarter of an hour later the intercom crackled and the pilot announced that they were now flying over the river where they would be fishing.

A grey-white band of unpolished silver wound westward in the green depths of the valley which cut through the terrain. A groove which cut right across Sweden.

'We're almost there now,' said the major.

Ten minutes later the plane descended and swept over the surface of the open lake which was the source of the river. The lower the plane flew, the higher the surrounding mountains became. Finally, they were completely surrounded by mountain giants except for where the river flowed out. It was as if they were landing in the bottom of a cauldron.

The plane approached the surface of the water. The waves slapped the pontoons an instant before the water engulfed them, and reduced the speed. Slowly the plane steered in towards land, where a lone man waved a greeting, waded out into the water, and grabbed one of the pontoons.

Haseke carried his secretary to shore through the shallow water, the baggage followed the same way, and the plane turned out towards the lake. They stood on the shore, watching the plane rise and disappear, until the silence was deafening.

They had landed by the lake's outlet, on the only low-lying stretch of beach. All around them, except for where they stood, the mountains plunged abruptly into the water. The major explained that the lake, called Paktasjärvi, was dammed and served as a reservoir for the power station about two hundred kilometres down the river. Its surface had been raised four metres, and this had flooded the natural shore. He had not planned to land in this virgin landscape: normally the helicopter would have brought the party right outside the lodge.

He introduced the man waiting for them on the shore, Grahn, the warden of Paktas Lodge and their host for the coming week. He was over fifty, but gave no impression of age—rather of a long and practical adjustment to a terrain where only resilient willows could rise above ground level. He was thin and wiry with a hooked nose, small mouth and a protruding chin. He wore a tyrolean hat, a grey-green anorak and a pair of worn corduroy trousers tucked into his boots.

'I apologize for the weather,' he said. 'But it does at least have the advantage that you'll be spared the mosquitoes. There's a bit to walk, a good bit in fact. It'll take about half an hour.'

He took a backpack and a suitcase in each hand. The others divided the bags between themselves, so that Fräulein Krämer didn't have to carry anything.

They followed the low-lying shore up to the dam, a concrete wall that spanned about thirty metres from the rocks on the shore where they were standing to the cliff on the other side. Nature had built most of the dam. The wall itself was almost like a concrete wedge across the furrow which the river had worn into the rock. Two strong gates harnessed the ancient waterfall and transformed it into a well-controlled water outflow.

'It's automatically regulated,' explained the major. 'Instead of the river overflowing in the spring and drying up in the autumn, the flow of water is the same all year. It's been proved to be best for the fish.'

The major had to shout to be heard over the roaring water.

They walked another hundred metres before the major stopped at the edge of the steep slope down towards the river valley.

'There's Paktas Lodge,' he said, and pointed at two grey roofs a few kilometres down the valley. 'That's where we'll be staying.'

'Fantastic,' said Doctor Haseke. 'The wilderness dream.'

'Wunderschön,' said Fräulein Krämer.

'It would have been better if it weren't raining,' said Grahn.

'There's no such thing as bad weather, except in cities,' said Haseke.

The major knew that Haseke was joking. He did not mind. Even if he preferred people to be serious in serious situations, he realized that a joke could often lighten the atmosphere.

The river wound directly westward in the depths of the valley until, after a few kilometres, it disappeared into an inaccessible canyon. Along the north side of the valley, tall, steep mountains raised their peaks and pinnacles as if they were earnest watchmen guarding against the polar winds and cold. In the south the mountains were gently sloping and rounded as if they welcomed the sun and the south wind.

On the north side the river followed the cliffs, which plunged directly down to the water and only left room for a few metres of rugged shore. The southern shore was even less inviting. It ascended slowly in gentle hills and long slopes towards the foot of the mountain. The gradually sloping valley, between the river and the mountain in the south, varied dramatically in width between a few hundred and a thousand metres. The greenery was dazzling, as in early spring, although it was the first week in August.

They began the descent into the valley on a stony path. The major walked behind Fräulein Krämer and noticed that she stepped just as anxiously and uneasily as if she had been walking through road works at home on Jungfernstieg in Hamburg.

The clouds thickened and the light faded. It was nearly dusk when they arrived in the valley. The path was gentler here and more easily passable, and they walked at a rapid pace with Grahn in the lead and the major at the rear. When they reached the top of a hill, the major saw a light shining in the window of a cottage.

The cottages lay next to each other with the gables facing towards the river and a gravel yard between them. The farthest building was the guest cottage, containing all the bedrooms lying off a main corridor. Grahn disappeared in there with the bags. The nearest building was the main cottage, which consisted of the kitchen, the dining room and two rooms for Grahn and the housekeeper.

The housekeeper greeted the guests in the dining room, which harked back to the good old days: floor, walls, ceiling, chairs and tables all made of pine; tablecloths and curtains made from a handwoven, rust, chequered material; rustic rag-rugs and a copper kettle as wall decorations. The housekeeper herself looked as if she dated back to the same time as the furnishings. Her hair was pinned up in a bun and she wore a handwoven dress and apron with a crisp white blouse. She had hefty arms, peasant legs and a figure like an old-fashioned milkpail.

She welcomed them sullenly and showed them to a table set with tea cups and sandwiches. Two people, the pretty journalist from Stockholm and her blond photographer, were already sitting there, waiting. The photographer glanced up at them over a four-storeyed cardhouse, which he had built out of crispbread. The major could tell that the housekeeper was annoyed.

'You should get the Sport brand,' said the photographer. 'This Delikatess is far too soft.'

'It's meant to be eaten, not played with,' said the major.

'You're all wrong. Wasa brand crispbread is the latest development in playthings. Buy Wasa brand crispbread and solve the problem of what to do when it rains.'

The housekeeper came with a breadbasket, tore down the cardhouse, and carried off the crispbread slices in the basket. The major introduced everyone. Haseke chuckled at the incident with the cardhouse while translating for his secretary what the photographer had said.

'We'll postpone showing you the river and fishing spots until tomorrow morning,' said the major, when everyone had tea in their cups and had started eating the sandwiches. 'Breakfast is at eight. We'll leave the introductory talk until then.'

He asked the housekeeper where the two Danes were. She pursed her mouth and said they'd gone to bed.

'How do we contact the outside world, if we need to?' said Haseke.

'By radio,' answered the major. 'We have a connection to the mountain radio system. It's an ordinary short-wave radio, the same as the police use in cars and on foot patrol. We can call the mountain rescue team in Kiruna at any time. And we have a hook-up every morning between eight and half past, if they want to reach us.'

'Does this kind of radio really have such a long range?'

'No. It works by relay stations. If we make a call here the relay station at Sangartjokko automatically starts up. It's at a height of 1570 metres and has a range great enough to reach Kiruna. You can relax, Doctor Haseke. If Hamburg wants you for something, they can reach you here.'

'Maybe I'd be more relaxed if they couldn't reach me!'

'I understand,' said the major. 'You're joking. Actually, it's absolutely essential for safety's sake to have a connection with the mountain rescue system. Someone could get sick, for example.'

They finished their meal and the major said goodnight to his guests. The housekeeper wanted a few words with him, so he lingered on in the dining room, while Grahn showed the others to their rooms.

'Yes, Major Nilsson,' said the housekeeper. 'It's about the Danish guests. I don't want to complain, but I don't feel I should have to put up with everything. They wouldn't let me enter and clean their rooms this morning. They said they'd make their own beds and didn't want anyone in there at all. Surely they don't have the right to decide about the rooms? I have my job to do, and it includes cleaning all the rooms.'

'It's probably best to let them have their way nonetheless. We can't afford any trouble. Everything must go smoothly and harmoniously, so that the guests get on well.'

He knew he sounded calm and authoritative. He was used to concealing his uneasiness. Uneasiness was exactly what he had felt about the two Danes, ever since he had met them at the station in Kiruna. Two travel experts travelling by train. Why hadn't they arrived by plane like the others? And the two bags that the big, strong one had been dragging and which he'd warned the major not to touch. They had seemed heavy enough to be filled with scrap iron. Neither of the men fitted in with his conceptions of how representatives of a large travel organization should behave.

That night before he fell asleep, he thought about the two Danes again. And while he slept, their two names echoed somewhere in his consciousness. They had an unpleasant and ominous sound.

Steiner and Moll.

4

IT WAS ONE of the most beautiful salmon trout Peter Baxter had ever seen. It was almost a metre long and ten centimetres wide across the back. It was covered with light brown spots like the sandy river bottom. A perfect camouflage. He would never have noticed the fish, had it not been for its dark shadow on the bottom, which moved back and forth as the fish rose and sank.

The sun had climbed over the ridge behind him in the south. He had woken before the others and gone straight down to the river with his fly rod in one hand, a box of flies in the other, and a net hanging from his belt. This was what he lived for: to wander along a stream in the wilds, alone with the water, mountains and sky. He felt one with the flowing river and the immovable landscape; a spark of life in lifeless surroundings. And fishing chased away his worst enemy: memories of the past.

Nowadays, the only place he felt good was in the wilderness. In the city, he felt as if every street were mined and each room set with trapdoors. He had run away from London with all its people and their sweat in the crowded underground, where they hung from the straps and swayed with the train's movements like seaweed in the waves of a polluted bay. He had taken the job at Kiruna to be as far away from home as possible. but his thoughts had followed him even there and forced him back to the ruins of his shattered happiness. Only nature left him in peace. There was nothing here to lead his thoughts back to what had been. And fishing demanded his complete concentration.

The trout had not seen him. It lay in the hollow behind a rock and continued rising and sinking. Carefully he stepped back, opened his box of flies, took out a March Brown and tied it on. Then he licked the gut leader, so that it would not stay afloat, but would draw the fly underneath the surface of the water and tempt the trout.

He made a rough estimate. The distance from the shore to the rock was three metres. He would need four metres of line, so that the fly would land in front of the rock and float downstream towards the fish. He stood so far back that the tip of the rod just reached the water. At all costs he must avoid alarming the fish with the shadow of the rod.

He drew out his line and cast. The fly made a slow arc in the air and fell into the water. Unsuccessful. Too near the rocks. The fly floated among the rocks of the shoreline. He reeled in the slack coils and carefully lifted the fly out of the water.

The trout was still there.

He took a deep breath and looked around to relax himself. Before him rose the sunlit mountain with alternating smooth cliffs, chaotic rock slides and grey, rugged areas which looked like elephant skin. In the west the mountains forming the border with Norway outlined their spiky contours against the sky, which was smooth and ice-blue like the inside of a pigeon's egg. The crystal-clear water rushed past in its endless marathon race to the sea.

More line was needed. He drew out about five metres and made a new cast. The fly landed on target, was drawn down into the water, followed the current and slipped closely past the rock, straight towards the trout. He held his breath. He could see everything in the clear water.

The trout glided away and let the fly float past. It appeared completely uninterested.

Suddenly it sprang to life. With a powerful stroke of its tail it dashed after the fly. Gaping. Then it shut its mouth on the fly.

Peter raised the tip of the rod and pulled gently in the opposite direction. The reel whirred as the fish, tearing off line, began its wild dash to the river's depths. It swam back and forth, jerking and tearing. Then it dove downwards and lay still.

He tested it carefully, raising the rod and increasing the pull on the line. Then it rose out of the water. A silent jump two metres up in the air.

Down with a splash.

Up again, with a thrashing tail and white spray of water. Then it took off upstream. After ten metres, it stopped.

The trout lay still once again.

Slowly Peter lifted the tip of the rod, until the coils of the line straightened out on the surface. The trout came up for the third time; jaw open, fins taut, the tail bent to one side, the classic picture of a jumping trout. Another belly flop. And off again towards the bottom.

After that, it was as if the fish had lost its wind. Its resistance weakened quickly. Peter began to reel in the line. After a few minutes the fish glided into the same hollow where he'd first noticed it. The fly was still hooked in the upper jaw.

He drew the fish into the shallows. It floated helplessly on its side. It did not react when it bumped into the stones on the bottom. It seemed half dead. Peter untied the net from his belt, approached the edge of the water, bent down and scooped up the fish. The game was over.

The water exploded. The fish burst up from the bottom. Thrashed with its tail. Heaved its body. Lashed with its head.

The leader snapped with the sound of a whip. The tip of the rod sprang up. The fish was free.

It swam slowly away from the shore. The last Peter saw of it was its broad tailfin waving from side to side. A taunting farewell.

He sank down into the grass along the shore and smiled at the water flowing past. He had fought an even battle and lost. He'd been outwitted in a moment of weakness. When he had been sure of his victory.

A voice penetrated the roar of the river. Someone was shouting behind him. He turned around and screwed up his eyes against the sun. Someone came walking down towards him in the bright light. He could not see who it was, but there was something familiar about the long hair and careless walk.

His heart stopped. He knew it was impossible, but the woman descending the slope was his wife Jane. Young and pretty, with her broad face, slender limbs, and familiar clothes: worn jeans, a chequered shirt and casual shoes.

He rose to his feet, and shadowing his eyes with his hand, he saw that of course it was not Jane. How could it be? It was the journalist from Stockholm.

'Too bad,' she said when she reached him. 'I was standing up there and saw the whole thing. What a performance! I didn't know they could jump so high.'

'Yes,' he said. 'No!'

'Was it a salmon trout? What happened? Did it get free?'

'Yes.'

Up close she was not particularly like Jane, her mouth was not so small, her eyes were not so large, and Jane had not had a single one of the many freckles which were sprinkled over this girl's nose.

'Breakfast is ready,' she said. 'I came down to get you.'

'That's kind of you,' he said.

He followed her up the slope. His legs were a little unsteady as always when memories engulfed him and he relived, yet again, how Jane had died on that sunny street corner in York, her head crushed right in front of his feet by a skidding lorry. They'd only been married for three days and were just taking a quick look at a Tudor house. A minute earlier they'd been laughing together.

'What's the matter?' asked the journalist. 'You look ill. Does losing a fish mean that much to you?'

'Fish?' he said, taken by surprise. 'What fish?'

She looked at him inquiringly. He dropped his fishing tackle, picked it up again and said he felt all right and that there were lots of fish in the stream; you caught some and not others, and therein lay the fascination of fishing.

The others were already sitting at the table when they entered the dining room and sat down next to each other in the only empty places at the short end of the table.

'I see you've already tried your luck at fishing,' the major greeted him. 'How was it?'

'Fine. I hooked one, a rather big one. But it got away.'

The smell of tea and toast filled the room, the sun shone through the windows and aroused in Peter a feeling of childhood, summer and freedom. Not a spot on the chequered tablecloths, not a scratch on the newly waxed floors, not a wrinkle in the floor mat; everything was new and unused. On one of the walls someone had indulged his taste for elks and blood-red sunsets by hanging up a picture with these ingredients.

The housekeeper came in, served Anna coffee and Peter tea and pointed out the three kinds of bread, the spicy sausage, the cheese and the eggs. She then asked if they'd prefer porridge the following morning, how they liked their eggs cooked, and if they'd noticed that they were meant to write their names on the napkin rings.

Breakfast passed with bits of conversation between the mouthfuls and gulps. Soon the cigarette smoke rose in the rays of sunshine. A feeling of well-being and fellowship began to spread, as it always does in a group of people among whom no one has yet expressed a difference of opinion which prevents the rest of the group from feeling that they agree about everything.

Peter wondered about the two Danes. Moll, the big, strong one, remained silent, staring at the tablecloth with his huge hands on his knees, looking as out of place as an old-time farm-worker who'd been invited to the squire's breakfast table.

His partner Steiner was more sociable and asked the major

questions in his odd combination of Danish and Swedish. He smoked a cigar, of course, and, being a true connoisseur, had brought a supply of his own Hirschprung. Cigarettes were a pleasure only fit for women and teenagers, he scoffed. Then he lit his cigar with the aid of a match he held in one hand, bringing the cigar towards the base of the flame with the other. When it was lit, he raised it to his mouth and blew a few puffs of smoke over the table, as if he were making a smokescreen. He apologized and laughed again. A typical commercial traveller's trick, thought Peter.

Grahn entered the dining room with a large sketch of the river and its nearest surroundings, which he hung up on the wall.

'Grahn will now brief you on the fishing,' said the major.

'Yes,' said Grahn. 'Nearest to us are four fishing pools.' He pointed to the four Roman numerals, a few hundred metres apart along the river.

'Where the pools end, there's an excellent area for stray fish,' he continued. 'It goes on for a few kilometres, before the river flows into the canyon. You can't get any farther. Farthest away there's a deserted Lapp hut in the middle of a lovely wood of mountain birch. Anyone can go in there to rest or take shelter from the rain. Once the hut was used frequently by the Lapps. There was a migratory trail through here, which came up from the lake, where you landed yesterday, went past the cabins, up into the mountains to the deserted hut and continued towards the woodlands through the pass behind Lektivagge. That's the mountain which forms the south side of the river's canyon. The route isn't used any more. Since the water level of the lake was raised with the construction of the dam, its shores have become inaccessible.'

'Have a go at the stray fish,' interrupted the major. 'That stretch is virtually unfished. There are lots of exciting little rapids and secret hollows. In some places the willow trees form a wall along the shore, so you can't fish there. But you can try wherever it's open behind you.'

'Yes,' said Grahn. 'Let's take the pools one by one. We call the first pool, the Cove.'

He pointed at the sharp bend in the river.

'Upstream from there it isn't really suitable for fishing.' He made a sweeping movement up towards the dam. 'We fish from the first pool downstream.'

'Upstream from the Cove, the fishing is poor,' said the major.

'We call the second pool, the Table Rock. A rock slab juts out into the water and it's handy for fishing off. Below the Table Rock the Grand Rapids start. That's also fine fishing, but it's a difficult stretch to get to. The willows grow right down to the edge of the water.'

He pointed to a wide strip of willow trees which were marked with crosses.

'The third pool is called the Creek. A creek runs into the river and that's a well-known guarantee of good fishing. The fourth pool is the Cauldron. To reach it, you have to make a detour around the willow thicket, but it's well worth the trouble. I've never left the Cauldron without having caught a fish. Well, those are the pools. Beyond them, there's the stray fish, as I said.'

'I'd like to add something,' said the major. 'No one should go into the mountains alone. We'll organize outings with Grahn as the guide for those who are interested.'

'Yes, you must be careful in the mountains. Even Linnaeus himself nearly got lost not far from here. Although it was two hundred years ago, nothing's really changed here since then.'

'Any questions?' asked the major.

'What time of day do the fish bite best?' asked the German director of the travel agency.

'In the evening, when the sun's gone down behind Paktasvagge Mountain,' replied Grahn. 'But they also bite well early in the morning. Really any time except in the middle of the day, if it's warm and sunny like today.'

He stood quietly for a while and looked expectantly at the group around the breakfast table. He had good reason to be satisfied with himself, Peter thought. If he were in a similar position next summer, he'd model his explanation on Grahn's. The sketch of the river, with the pools clearly marked, was especially worth copying.

'Well,' Grahn said. 'Let's go then. If anyone doesn't have his own rod, he can borrow one from me.'

'Hey,' said the journalist to Peter. 'What's that knife Grahn has in his belt?'

'It's a Lapp knife,' he answered. 'A very fine one too. The pattern on the sheath is of pagan origin. The blade itself was probably cut by a circular sword blade.'

He stopped talking. He'd become aware of her scent which brought on a surge of awful memories. He wondered what was the matter with him and why he couldn't rid himself of the ghosts from his past.

5

WHEN EVERYONE HAD left the main cottage, the housekeeper settled down with a cup of coffee and two substantial sandwiches, one with liver sausage and the other with ham. She could not understand women who were so obsessed with the modern ideal of slenderness that they preferred enduring a mass of neuroses rather than a few extra kilos around their waists. Outside the brave fishermen walked past on their way to the river. She did not understand them either. These grown-up men who had nothing better to do than to stand by a river day in day out. And at what cost? The fish caught here must be the most expensive food in the world if one added up all the costs: the flight, food and accommodation, lost wages. The price per kilo must be at least two hundred kroner. Of course, they would bring their catch to her and she would have to clean and scale the wretched things. She knew from experience that eating their fish was just as much of a ritual for these fisherman as taking Holy Communion was for a priest.

The housekeeper cleared the table. She had to do the washing up by hand. No electricity meant no dishwasher. The refrigerator, cooker and hot-water heater ran on bottled gas like the central heating.

She carried the overloaded tray to the kitchen, put all the leftovers in the refrigerator and breadbin, then brought in another overloaded tray, this time laden with china. She filled the basin with warm water, squirted in some washing-up liquid and set to work. She placed all the dishes in the drying rack, except for one coffee cup, which she wiped with paper towelling to remove a red mark. Lipstick in the wilderness. She grimaced. It must have been that German woman.

The kitchen, with its broad surfaces and roomy cupboards, was a pleasant place to work. It was bright and cosy and had windows in both the short walls, to the west facing the border mountains and to the east facing the yard and guest cottage. If she opened the door of her room, she could see right down to the river. Both her room and Grahn's lay in the gabled ends of the building, opening on to the kitchen.

She dried her hands and went into her room. She sat in the only armchair and stared at the river. The group was just coming from the first pool to the Table Rock, the only part of the river which was visible from the cottage. The photographer and journalist from Stockholm were not with them. Obviously, they had been posted at the Cove. She saw Grahn pointing at the river and giving a rod to one of the Danes, who remained behind when the others continued on to the next pool.

She put out her cigarette and entered the linen storeroom, which also opened on to the kitchen opposite Grahn's room. She took out eight hand towels, one for each guest, and went over to the guest cottage.

When she opened the door of the first room, she wondered, for an instant, if a ladies' clothing salesman had unpacked his goods there. The room was strewn with clothes. Dresses, skirts, trousers, blouses and jumpers were hanging on any protruding objects, on doorknobs, cupboard handles, and mirrors. The German woman certainly had not skimped on baggage. There was no trace of the doctor except his pyjamas lying on the unmade bed. His secretary dominated the room. Some secretary. Perhaps he liked dictating his letters in bed . . .

The housekeeper opened the top drawer of the dresser. Just as she had suspected. Ragged bras and laddered tights. She knew what elegance looked like under the surface. A lifetime of working in hotels had taught her that. She remembered once reading that the great Swedenborg had never washed because he believed that nothing as worldly as dirt could possibly settle on his holy body. Young women certainly couldn't excuse their uncleanliness with holy souls. It was plain, simple dirtiness; nothing else.

She stripped the bed, then entered the bathroom where she wiped spots of mascara off the washbowl, picked up pieces of cotton wool from the floor, and changed the towels. Then she made the bed, put on the bedspread, and went on to the next room.

It was the major's. He had not had the energy to put the whisky bottle back in the cupboard. She did not mind his having a glass or two, if only he would clear up afterwards. She suspected though, that a glass or two was not quite enough for the major.

The next room was locked and the key was not on the hook by the door. Then she remembered. This room belonged to those peculiar Danes. She'd been forbidden to go in here. And to top it off, they had had the cheek to take the key with them. Surely they didn't think she would stand for that!

She took the major's key and opened the door. All the keys fit all the doors; the Danes did not know it, but she did. She had the right to enter any room she pleased. As well as the responsibility. It was her duty to clean and tidy everywhere.

Just as she had thought! Neither of them had made their beds. She opened the window to air the stuffy room while she made the beds. She put on a bedspread and changed the towels in the bathroom.

It was then she noticed the bags, which the big Dane had been dragging as if he were training for a great test of strength. She tried to lift one. It must weigh more than forty kilos. She put it down and opened it.

It was full of white boxes, lying side by side, with their lids facing upwards. Eight boxes. She took the lid off one and discovered ten yellow sticks, or cylinders, that looked as if they were made of wax. There was a faint smell of vanilla.

What were they? Sticks of plasticine? Suddenly it dawned on her. She'd seen something similar during her time as a housekeeper at the officers' mess in Boden. It was gelignite, lots of gelignite. There was enough here to blow up both the cottage and herself as well. Good God! What should she do?

She must get hold of Grahn and the major!

At that moment she heard footsteps in the corridor. The door opened. When she saw who it was, she was about to let fly with questions and complaints. But the words stuck in her throat. Something about his eyes made her stiffen with fear. And the way he held his hand.

He held it raised diagonally in front of him like a club.

6

Everything was under control. Grahn watched Peter Baxter standing by the shore of the Cauldron, the last pool, and rigging his rod. Baxter seemed to be a skilful fisherman, a bit shy perhaps to be a good guide, but he would soon get over that. Grahn was pleased and contented. Everyone was posted by the river, they had been given their instructions; now it was just a question of time before they caught the fish. He had never seen any water with a greater abundance of fish so eager to bite.

The path through the lush grass went straight up the slope and in a wide curve around a thick wood of willows, before it turned back towards the river to the third pool, the Creek, about half a kilometre upstream.

Grahn relaxed and enjoyed the birds' singing, which could be heard more clearly as the river's roar grew fainter. It was midday and the valley had become a sun-trap. The buttercups strained upwards to reach above the other flowers in the meadow. The mountains were blue in the distance. Not a breath of wind. Not a mosquito. This was paradise.

Grahn had arranged his life perfectly. He had succeeded in making his interests into his career. In the winter he skied and in the summer he fished. Professionally. He took advantage of precipitation in all its forms, snow on the mountains in winter, melted snow in creeks and rivers in the summer. He worked as an expedition leader and ski guide in the frontier from January to April and as a warden at a fishing lodge from June to September.

A wheatear flew up in front of him on his way past the edge of the jungle of bushes. The Lappsparrows quarrelled in the willowtops and had no time to be disturbed. Far ahead, on the other side of the river, the crown of Paktasvagge had been powdered white during the night. The highest cliff was wreathed with clouds like the head of Zeus. Even higher soared a bird with an enormous wing span. A golden eagle or a white-tailed eagle maybe. Grahn could not tell which one; the distance was too great. At closer range he could easily tell them apart. He knew nearly everything about the natural world around him. Linnaeus had once said that you can only enjoy something you know about —you are blind to what you do not know. Linnaeus was always right.

On the other side of the willow thicket the river roared on like a never-ending train. There was something special about this river.

It was his river.

In the last ten years he had been in many different fishing lodges, at Rostojaure, Sinotjaure, Tjonajokk and elsewhere, but always as an assistant. Paktasvagge was his first job as warden entirely on his own. He smiled to himself. King of the Paktas valley. King for the summer. Maybe more. Perhaps he could make himself indispensable.

He put his thoughts aside. The past was already lost. He did not yet own the future. Only the present was completely his. He had never been the type of person who spent half his life waiting for something to happen and the other half missing what had been. He lived in the present, amongst snow-covered summits, blossoming mountain meadows and rushing water.

The path completed its half curve around the willows and reached the creek, which cascaded playfully, splashing and foaming its way down from the rocks into the sun of the south. There were no more willows and the path followed along the creek and meandered down to the river and to the third pool.

Grahn saw Haseke standing out in the water, submerged to the tops of his waders. On the shore the major was wandering back and forth. Fräulein Krämer sat on a rock, her eyes closed and her face towards the sun. She had rolled up her sleeves and opened the top of her blouse.

'How's it going?' Grahn asked the major.

The major was startled. He had not heard Grahn approaching.

'Oh, it's Grahn,' he said. 'What? Oh well, nothing. Not even a strike. Didn't you say they always bite here? Maybe he's fishing incorrectly.'

But Grahn could see that Haseke was not fishing incorrectly. He was an expert fly-fisherman. He let the rod sway back and forth through the air so that the line curved in gentle whiplashes, now in front of him, now behind him. At each extreme he let out a little more line. His cast was perfect.

Then he extended the rod with his arm stretched out completely. The fly flew gently through the air and landed right at the edge of the backwater formed where the creek flowed into the river. The backwater consisted of a shiny stream slowly flowing within the more rapid mainstream.

The fly floated forward without any result. Haseke lifted it up out of the water just before it got to the farthest point.

He began false casting with a wrist movement that looked as if he were painting the underside of the roof. This time, he placed the fly farther forward and out into the backwater, just one metre from the main course of the current.

The pink dry fly floating slowly over the water's dark surface looked like an orchid carried across a lagoon by gentle wind.

Suddenly it disappeared. Sucked down into the water. Swallowed. A violent ripple, a backfin sliced through the water surface, a thrashing tailfin.

Haseke lifted up the tip of the rod in a definite counter-jerk. The fish was hooked.

Grahn felt the major grasp his arm.

'Take it easy, major,' said Grahn. 'He knows his stuff.'

The fish took the line. It went out into the main current and let itself be swept along. It stopped and sulked. Haseke raised the tip of the rod to get it fighting again. He worked the fish hard.

Up came the fish out of the water. Its bent back flashed in the sun before it fell back with a spraying belly flop. Haseke was playing with a taut line and steady resistance.

The fish tired and Haseke began to reel in the line. He raised the tip of the rod, dropped it quickly and reeled in. The fish moved towards the shore near the end of the backwater about thirty metres downstream.

Haseke turned around.

'Net!'

Grahn picked up his net from the grass, walked past Fräulein Krämer, who was now standing to watch the performance out in the river, continued along the river bank and stood ready with the net.

The fish came through the water, gliding on its side—lovely salmon trout of about two kilos, firmly hooked in its lower jaw. It was tired now. Dead tired.

Carefully he passed the net under the fish and lifted it out of the water. He drew his knife, held it by the tip and dealt a blow with the handle right between the fish's eyes. It died instantaneously.

Grahn cut the fly off the leader and let the line drift back out into the water. Haseke began to reel in immediately. He looked at the fly in the fish's jaw. It was a Red Quill, size ten.

Grahn returned with the fish in hand at the same time as Haseke waded ashore. Fräulein Krämer approached with an expression of both curiosity and disappointment: curiosity about the object which was the main reason for the long trip from Germany; disappointment over the fact that it was, after all, just another dead fish. Grahn knew from experience that women never expressed enthusiasm for men's catches. At most, they showed indulgence towards the childishness of their men. Women did not understand that there was something the matter with them. They had never really been children.

Haseke weighed the fish on a spring balance. Two point two kilos. He laughed.

'A fine fish,' he said.

He laughed even more heartily. It was as if a dam had burst, a dam of responsibility and efficiency built up over the years Now happiness gushed forth, warm and boyish. Grahn had seen it happen many times. Dignified men with stern faces turning into lively boys. He began to like the German. Fräulein Krämer returned to her rock and sunbathing.

'It couldn't have begun better,' said Haseke. 'I've fished lots of places, but it's never started this successfully.'

He unfastened the fly from the fish's mouth and put it to dry on a flat stone. He took a flat wooden box out of his tackle bag and opened it. In it dry flies paraded in gaudy ranks like miniature natives on the warpath. Black Gnat with its bristly body and grey wings; March Brown with its silver body and brown wings; the red and white Royal Coachman; Wickham's Fancy; Greenwell's Glory; all with imaginative names like race horses.

Grahn observed Haseke's tackle with an expert's appreciation for perfect equipment: the fine old three-piece split bamboo rod made out of glued bamboo cane and brass guides; the Hardy reel; the double-tapered line; the flies all in perfect condition.

'What about a beer?' he asked.

'Grahn, what do you mean? Why should we leave now when they've just started biting?'

'No,' said Grahn. 'Let's stay here. Let me invite you to the Adler Hotel,'

'Adler?'

Grahn pointed at some rocks which were just the right height for sitting on. He bowed deeply, imitating an old-fashioned servant.

'Ladies and gentlemen, here you are. Drinks will be served in a moment.'

He went to the creek, above where it flowed into the river, bent down and drew up a white plastic bucket wedged between two rocks in the water. He hung the bucket over one arm and with exaggerated dignity walked back to the group. He laughed at himself. He was playing the lead role in a comedy he had created, but at the same time he was part of the audience and enjoyed the effect his performance had on his guests.

The major looked perturbed. Haseke explained in German to his secretary that she was now seated at the Adler Hotel.

Grahn removed the lid of the bucket and picked out a can of Tuborg Export. He pulled the tab and offered the can to Fräulein Krämer.

'Madame,' he said, and bowed with his hand in front of his waist. The only words he knew in German were danke schön, which was inappropriate.

He served the men each a can of beer, pulled out a piece of smoked sausage from the bottom of the bucket, cut a slice for each person and offered them around. Then he settled down on a rock next to the others and raised his own can of beer:

'Skoal!' he said to Haseke. 'Here's to your first fish in the mountains of Sweden. Expertly caught!'

'What organization,' smiled Haseke. 'What a reception. Such a surprise. Thank you, gentlemen!'

'It's begun well,' said Grahn, when everyone was chewing and drinking.

'I remember one time on the Atla River,' said the major. 'We arrived by car, having driven a short distance from Lyngen, very early in the morning. I couldn't resist the temptation. I went straight down to the river, prepared my rod and made a cast. A strike straight away. Ten minutes later I was back in the yard where the others were unloading their bags. Imagine their surprise when I showed them the salmon. It wasn't small either. Seven and a half kilos. We fished there for three days and nights and didn't see another fin.'

'Amazing,' said Haseke. 'The same thing happened to me with my first swordfish. Have any of you fished in the Indian Ocean? This was on the island of Mafia off the east coast of Africa. You fly there in half an hour from Dar-es-Salaam and stay in a modern lodge right by the shore of Chole Bay. Well, I landed on the airstrip, jogged across the island in a landrover, left my bags in reception and got straight on to the boat. In ten minutes we were out by Kinhasi Pass, the only opening in the coral reef. I cast out my bait, a piece of fish fastened on to a strong hook. I'd no sooner strapped myself in my chair, than I saw a stick thrust up out of the water where the bait dragged behind the boat. I let the line run out and the bait looked like a dead fish on the surface of the water. Then the swordfish swallowed the bait and hook. The battle was fantastic. The fish came up out of the water and danced on its tail for over a hundred metres while thrashing with its sword to free itself from the line. Then it dived into the deep. And up again. It took exactly an hour and four minutes to get it into the boat. Since then, I've been to Mafia three times. I've caught lots of fish there, but never another swordfish.'

'Unfortunately we can't offer you swordfish here,' said the major stiffly.

'Oh,' said Haseke. 'Of course, I don't expect it. In my opinion, your salmon trout measure up to any fish in the Indian Ocean. Even swordfish.'

Grahn's well-being was at its peak. Everything had worked out perfectly. Everything was at its best. The weather, the fishing, the people. The mosquitoes had not appeared at all. And that restaurant gimmick had really hit the mark. In such a performance it was that little something extra, that unexpected detail that made all the difference.

'Schatze,' said Fräulein Krämer. 'Guck mal! Was ist das draussen im Wasser?'

She pointed towards an object floating in the water.

At first Grahn did not grasp what he saw. Was it a sack? Then he recognized the striped clothes as something he'd seen before; but where? He stood up to get a better look. Instantly he understood. It was a body floating out there.

'Good God!' he exclaimed.

'What is it?' asked the major.

'The housekeeper. There must have been an accident. We must get her ashore!'

Grahn ran out into the water. Then he stopped himself and returned to shore. The backwater was too deep for him to wade out and rescue the housekeeper's body. And the water was too cold for him to swim.

'We must get her up here,' said the major. 'And bloody fast! If she floats out of the backwater, we'll never see her again.'

'Right,' said Grahn.

The shore below the backwater was inaccessible. The willows grew right down into the water.

Out in the water the body drifted on, slowly spinning around and around.

'Do something, damn it!' shouted the major.

Suddenly Haseke came to life.

He turned the tackle bag upside down, opened a plastic box

which clattered on to the rocks, took a spinner from the box and tied it on to the empty leader on his fishing line. Then he set his thumb against the reel, raised the rod behind him and cast.

The spinner flew through the air. Silently it hit the water a few metres beyond the drifting body, so that the line fell across the striped apron. He began to reel in. The body moved. The spinner had fastened. The hook had caught hold.

Testingly, he raised the tip of the rod. The line grew taut, the body ceased drifting, and lay still in the water. Carefully he increased the pressure. Slowly the body started to move towards land.

'Come,' said Grahn to the major and began walking along the shore. The major followed him. Out in the river, the dead body glided nearer and nearer to shore, hooked on Haseke's line and spinner.

Grahn stopped where he had netted Haseke's trout only half an hour ago. He waded out into the water. The body floated with its back facing upwards. The dark hair swayed like seaweed in the current. The bare arms and legs seemed luminous in the water.

He grabbed one hand and began to draw the body to shore. In the shallows the downturned face scraped against a rock on the bottom. He turned over the body and suddenly Ellen's eyes stared at him, dead and unseeing.

In an instant the major was beside him, detaching the spinner which had caught her skirt. Then he took her ankles and Grahn lifted under her shoulders, but the limp arms fell away so that he could not get a good grip. He then took hold of her wrists. Staggering over the rocks, they carried the housekeeper's body ashore.

She lay on her back with her eyes staring up at the sky. Her lower jaw hung open; water filled her mouth.

A phrase drifted into Grahn's mind, he did not know from where, but it repeated itself again and again: matter which does not breathe is dead matter. Matter which does not breathe is dead matter. Matter which does not breathe is dead matter.

In the distance he heard Fräulein Krämer crying.

7

THE DAY HAD lost its brilliance. The sun shone like a spotlight on the lifeless scene. The mountains stood cold and indifferent against an empty sky. Grahn thought of a poem by Mao Tse Tung which he'd once read:

> Mountain!
> Peaks pierce the blue sky
> Unblunted.
> Without the mountain's support
> The sky would fall.

He sat next to the major on the bench outside the workshop. Combining their strength, they had carried the housekeeper's body up to the house and put it in the workshop situated under the kitchen of the main cottage. The major had set up a camp bed, where they'd laid her, and Grahn had covered her with a sheet from the linen storeroom. Haseke was taking care of Fräulein Krämer. Both the Danes had found out about the accident when they had seen Grahn and the major carrying the body. They had immediately set out for the first pool to inform the photographer and journalist.

Grahn was tired from the great strain of carrying the housekeeper's body up to the house and he heard the major breathing heavily next to him on the bench. The housekeeper's death meant chaos. Without her, the services could not function. Which meant dissatisfied guests. Which, in turn, meant that the German contract was jeopardized and they risked bad publicity. What would happen to him? He quickly dismissed the thought. It certainly could not be worse for him than it had been for Ellen. Only a few hours ago she had been in the kitchen in the midst of her daily chores. And now, there she was, lying under a sheet in the workshop.

'I wonder how she fell into the water,' he said. 'What could she have been doing by the river?'

The major cleared his throat. He straightened his back as if the former officer within him had ordered the present discouraged civilian to pull himself together and exert some self-discipline. He looked at Grahn with a determined expression.

'Those questions will have to wait until we've dealt with two things: first of all, we must inform the police and authorities; secondly, we must offer some food and drink to our guests. Food is important in keeping up one's spirits. An army marches on its stomach, Napoleon once said. That also goes for tourists in the wilderness. Especially if they've just experienced a shock.'

They entered the main cottage, passed through the kitchen and stood in front of the radio in Grahn's room.

'What should I say?'

'Just report a death. Ask for any necessary instructions. The police know what to do.'

Grahn switched on the radio, took the microphone in his hand and began to speak.

'It seems dead,' he said.

He switched it on and off a few times without any result. He went over to his dresser, opened the top drawer, took out some new batteries and replaced the old ones. No improvement. Still no life in the radio.

'Odd,' he said.

'Doesn't the equipment work?' asked the major. 'What carelessness! Try again!'

Grahn checked all the loose parts of the apparatus. He couldn't find anything wrong. He couldn't get it to work either.

'Damned bad luck,' he said, bewildered. 'That it should break down just now.'

'Bad luck?'

'It worked perfectly this morning when I spoke to Kiruna.'

'You call it bad luck; I call it a catastrophe. Do you know what this means? We'll be stuck with the housekeeper's corpse in the workshop for a whole week. A catastrophe, I call it, a catastrophe.'

'Yes,' agreed Grahn.

'And we're one hundred kilometres away from the nearest settlement. Christ.'

'It isn't really as bad as that. There's a fishing lodge some kilometres down the river which belongs to the National Board of Crown Foresets and Lands. They use it for entertainment purposes.'

'But that's not possible!' The major grew even more upset. 'We guarantee absolute isolation and at least one hundred kilometres' distance to the nearest settlement, and it turns out that there are people much closer than that. What a scandal!'

'It isn't as bad as it sounds. The lodge isn't on the map. It's used as a retreat for visiting foreign heads of state who want some peace and quiet. Kekkonen has fished here many times, our own King too, for that matter. Last summer he spent a week there. I don't think our guests would ever get in touch with the inhabitants of the other fishing lodge.'

'Can you find your way there?'

'Yes, I can. I know where the lodge is. Along the river, about twenty kilometres downstream. But you can't go along the river; it's inaccessible that way. You've got to follow the old trail and go up the mountain behind Lektivagge.'

He brought out a map from another drawer and spread it out on the desk.

'Look here,' he said, pointing to the river where it disappeared into a ravine below their valley. 'Here's the deserted Lapp hut. The trail leads from there up to this plateau, continues south to avoid the marshlands here, and turns due east through the pass between Lektivagge and the mountain behind here. Then the trail continues in a curve back towards the river. The other lodge is situated just about where the trail meets the river again.'

'It doesn't seem too difficult.'

'The problem is following the trail. It hasn't been used in many years and it isn't marked. Many stretches are overgrown. And if you miss the trail, you could easily get lost in the mountains. Especially if the visibility is poor.'

'Can you manage it?'

'I think so.'

'How long will it take?'

'That's hard to say. Six, or seven hours, maybe eight, maybe more.'

'Is there a radio there?'

'There's everything. And right now the place is in full operation. I know Allan Petterson, the warden there. I met him a week ago in Kiruna. They were receiving some important foreigner, he said. Of course, he's used to it. The government often drags people there to impress them with the Swedish wilderness. But this was something extra special. A big shot from England. He didn't know who it was. It was a great secret. Naturally, he didn't even say the visitor was from England, but I figured it out because Allan was in Kiruna to brush up on his English. Wait, when were the guests due to arrive? Tomorrow, I think. So he'll be busy preparing for them today. I'm sure we'll get some help.'

'Good. It's eleven o'clock now. If you leave at once, you'll reach there by six or seven. You'll alert the police in Kiruna immediately and the helicopter should be here around eight. It'll have to do.'

'I'll do my best.'

'I have complete confidence in you. Another important thing. Ask the police to contact Holm, the tourist director. The future of the scheme depends on it. We must have a replacement for the housekeeper. Quickly. Or else we can't stay on here. If the worst comes to the worst, Holm will have to send someone from Kebnekaise or another tourist resort. By plane, of course.'

'I'll deliver the message.'

'I hope you realize that everything depends on you. I'm counting on you.'

Grahn felt the paternal hand weighing heavily on his shoulder, but was careful not to smile. The major's sense of the moment's seriousness left no room for smiles.

The major left the room. Grahn brought out his backpack from the wardrobe and packed it with two pairs of socks, a pair of light climbing boots, an extra vest and a windproof anorak. Then he went into the kitchen, took a loaf of bread, some butter, a piece of cheese, a jar of coffee with a plastic top, a coffee pot, two boxes of matches and a plastic mug. He stuffed everything into a plastic bag and put the plastic bag into the pack. He was ready to set out.

Out in the yard he met the major, the two Danes, the photographer and the journalist. The major examined a blue plastic bucket which Steiner was holding up while he explained something.

'We found this on the way to the first pool. It lay by the edge of the shore. We thought it might have something to do with the accident.'

Grahn recognized the bucket without a doubt. It came from the kitchen and was kept in the cleaning cupboard.

'It's the housekeeper's bucket,' he said.

'Perhaps she went down to the river to fetch some water,' suggested the major. 'Then she slipped and fell in.'

'Why should she go to get water from the river,' asked Grahn, 'when she could use the taps up here?'

'Maybe she was picking berries,' suggested Steiner.

'I'm going now,' said Grahn.

He turned his back on them and overheard the major explaining where Grahn was going and why. The last thing he heard was the major telling what had happened to the radio with the well-chosen words: misfortunes seldom come singly. He was grateful for that. In that way adverse fate was blamed for the broken radio and not himself.

He began to walk along the path down the slope to the river. As soon as he felt there were no more eyes fixed on his back, he began to relax. The sound of the river's roar helped him recover his calm.

He looked back one last time and saw both the cottages and the people in the yard between them. Everything would be all right. He would reach Allan and the lodge that evening, the police would fetch the housekeeper's body, a new housekeeper would come and take care of the guests' temporary needs. Everything would return to normal. Ellen's death would become just another memory. An affirmation of the fact that in the end everything works out for the best, even if it looks bleak at the moment.

He remembered how a few years ago at a lodge near the frontier, he had sat next to a fellow at the lunch table, who had been joking and happy about the fine weather, but later that afternoon had got caught in an avalanche and broken his neck. That evening the general mood had been oppressive. But already the next day, a new guest had taken the dead man's place at the table. He was just as funny and the weather was just as fine.

He had not known Ellen. He had kept his distance as he did with all women. Once she had offered to sew on his buttons and mend a hole in his coat. He had declined. He knew that a woman's concern was just the first step in her attempt to gain control. He had never had much faith in the blessings of marriage. When two people became one, each one was necessarily reduced to a half.

He crossed the creek near the backwater and followed the path around the wide willow thicket. He thought of Peter Baxter. No one had thought to inform him about what had happened. He was still fishing at the Cauldron. Grahn spotted him as he came around the willows and the path veered back towards the river. For an instant he considered going down to talk to Baxter, but then he changed his mind. He had no time to lose. When the path forked he continued straight on beyond the Cauldron.

Gradually his good mood returned. He enjoyed exercise and feeling the blood pulse through his veins. He lengthened his stride. A path in the wilderness was his native heath. He looked forward to the long walk ahead, to climbing the heights and seeing once again the landscape spread out far below him, after his long stay in the valley. Up in the mountains he could see everything in its proper perspective. Nowhere was man's insignificance more apparent.

The path rambled over some boulders and then wound into a birchwood, where the trees stood spaced evenly apart as in an orchard. Between the motionless leaves the still air was filled with the smell of the mountain birch. Blueberry bushes grew between the slender white trunks. The berries were still unripe.

At the top of the glade, which ended by the whirling water of the river, stood the deserted Lapp hut. It was made from peat, in a standard ancient design, as old as mankind itself. Over a frame of birch, the roof and walls had been made from turf and earth. He had been here two days ago to cut fresh birch twigs for the floor. Everything was ready for the guests. There was a fireplace inside the hut and one outside too, as well as dry firewood and matches to light the fire.

He built a fire outside the hut, went down to the river to fill the coffee pot with water, poured in the ground coffee and set it on the fire. He made some sandwiches and waited for the coffee to boil. A quick meal in peace and quiet was a necessary preparation for the long walk ahead.

Suddenly he heard a noise penetrate the roar of the river and the birds' singing.

Footsteps.

Someone was walking on the path behind him.

He was startled, turned around, and was even more surprised when he saw who it was. But he did not let it show. He wanted to pick his own role in this drama, preferably the leading one.

He stood up and waved his hand.

'Welcome to the Coffee Hut,' he said. 'Do sit down. The coffee's just ready.'

He bent over to take the coffee pot from the fire.

He did not hear the quick steps behind his back; he did not see the arm raised ready to strike; he did not feel the blow striking his neck. It all happened too fast.

Naturally, he did not notice being carried into the hut and dumped on the twig-covered floor.

By then, he was already dead.

8

KEN COLLECTED KICKS. He did not know exactly what a kick was, except that in that culminating instant, everything came together. To eat breakfast in London, lunch in Paris and dinner in Barcelona, all on the same day, could be a kick, especially if the lobster at Caracoles was perfect. Or to get a little drunk on *retsina* one evening in the Plaka, the old town of Athens. Or to sit at Ramses in Cairo, where there were no tourists, and watch Egyptian women dancing in their scarves and beads and hear the men singing with such intensity that the audience rose out of their seats.

But most of all he got the biggest kicks from his job. They came at the moment when everything came together: the lighting, the background, and the girl, or whatever was in front of the camera. In that instant the unique quality, which would distinguish the picture from all others, was born. The world was full of mediocre photographers. It was too much work to compete with them. He kept himself in the rank above.

Even if he could not exactly define what a kick was, he could always tell when one was coming and steer it on to the right track. Right now, there was a kick well under way. He was going to take the perfect photograph of a fish.

Only half an hour ago, taking pictures had seemed completely out of the question. The atmosphere during lunch, which had been improvised in the kitchen, had been dominated by the fact that the person who should have prepared the meal was absent; but at the same time hauntingly present, since she lay directly below the kitchen floor, down in the workshop. The group had split up. Peter Baxter had not even appeared. Moll had gone to his room and, after making six sandwiches, Steiner had disappeared as well. Fräulein Krämer stayed in her room, letting herself be nursed by her doctor and boss.

But suddenly taking pictures had become necessary. At least, the major had made it seem so, when he asked to speak to Ken alone. It was crucial to keep the guests occupied, he said, and especially Doctor Haseke. Otherwise there was the risk that they would all leave as soon as contact was re-established with the outside world. The major was convinced that Fräulein Krämer had an unfortunate influence on Haseke. He must be kept busy. Could not Ken help? Could not he start photographing the fishing in the river with Haseke playing the main role?

'I'll be glad to help you,' Ken had replied. 'Free of charge. But you'll have to pay for the pictures, of course.'

'How much?'

'Well, I'm not one of those photographers who works for a Gustav II Adolf. I never do any work for less than Mother Sweden.'

'Pardon?'

'Haven't you ever looked at your banknotes? You'll find Gustav Adolf on the hundred kroner note; Mother Sweden is worth ten times as much.'

Ken had always found it easier to discuss serious matters if he disguised them as jokes. The joke provided the serious issue with a kind of self-lubricating ball-bearing, so that it could quickly slip into the conversation and then disappear again just as quickly. Money was a serious matter. Much more serious here in Sweden than it was at home. For most Swedes money was a subject which was discussed only among a select few. They treated their money as the bourgeoisie of earlier times had treated their mistresses: they kept completely silent about them outwardly but boasted within an inner circle.

He and the major had quickly come to an agreement. He would do an illustrated report on fishing in the river with the German as the main character for a Mother Sweden.

Later he had knocked at Anna's door. He had asked her to have a talk with Haseke. As there was the risk that the German would remain imprisoned by the bonds of feminine tears, he felt it would be a good idea to organize a counter-attack. Anna was easily persuaded.

'Look here, baby,' he had said. 'You've got an article to write about how Sweden is selling its wilderness to the Germans! You won't be able to do it if the Germans go home. A poor housekeeper drowned in the empty wilds means nothing compared with *Veckan Runt*. Put some coals on the fire and help get those hamburgers cooking!'

They walked down to the Cove in single file. Ken had spent the morning by the first pool and he already knew just about how he would take the photos. Ken went first with his camera bag over his shoulder, followed by the major and Anna, and last of all came Haseke and his secretary. Fräulein Krämer had regained her equilibrium after the shock of the housekeeper's death. Ken thought one could describe her condition with the same phrase he used when ordering a martini: stirred, but not shaken.

'This is how I see it,' he said, when they reached the river. 'Main photo: Doctor Haseke with a jumping trout. Difficulty: the great distance between both participants, the doctor and the fish. The distance must be reduced. We'll do that by placing the doctor and the fish in a direct line with the camera.'

Ken pointed out into the water. The Cove was true to its name: the pool consisted of two protruding rocks and a wide indentation between them, much like a quiet cove on the Riviera.

'You stand out in the water beyond the rock below the Cove. That way there'll be lots of water between us. When you get a bite, try to manoeuvre the fish into the Cove. Then I'll get my chance.'

'There's yet another difficulty you haven't mentioned,' said Haseke. 'I might not get a bite.'

'Don't worry,' said the major reassuringly. 'Remember you're fishing in one of the world's greatest trout streams.'

'But it might take a while,' said Ken. 'Major, while we're waiting, it'd be terrific if you'd help me with a picture I'd like to take. A cosy instructional picture. Stand with Anna out in the water and give her a lesson.'

They started. Haseke wandered up to the upper part of the Cove. The major began preparing his rod. Ken put a roll of Ektachrome X in each camera and chose the lenses, picking an 85mm telephoto lens for one and a moderately wide-angled 35mm lens for the other. He measured the light through both viewfinders and got the same result: a hundred and twenty-fifth of a second and an aperture of sixteen. He would need the smallest aperture possible to get the right depth of field.

Haseke had already cast his fly into the current by the time the major and Anna were wading out into the shallow water. Fräulein Krämer had arranged herself on a rock, copying the pose of the statue of The Little Mermaid, based on the fairytale by Hans Christian Andersen, which adorns the harbour in Copenhagen. Ken laughed when he saw her. The role of the bathing beauty by a river in Norrland did not suit her. That girl belonged in Pampelonne, Tahiti, Voile Rouge or some of the other beaches in St Tropez with parasols, deckchairs and waiters hurrying across the sand carrying gaily-coloured drinks.

The major placed the rod in Anna's hands.

'Feet apart,' he said. 'Left foot facing the direction of the cast. Hold the rod firmly in your right hand. Thumb straight. Leader in your left hand. Like that. Pull out a little line from the reel.'

Ken slung the camera with the telephoto lens around his neck, raised the other camera to his eye and began to focus through the wide-angle lens. The major stood behind Anna with his arms around her and had a good grip on her hands while he instructed her. There was something intimate about the scene, Ken thought. The Sultan of Norrland and his young slave, a ballet in two acts. Act One: the first time I took you out into the river.... He felt his spirits rising; he started taking photographs.

'Look here,' said the major. 'Raise your arm and snap your wrist so that the rod points straight upwards. Let the line extend its full length backwards. Then bring the rod forward, and let the fly drop into the water.'

Ken put Anna and the major into the frame, so that the rod formed a diagonal line from the lower left-hand corner to the upper right-hand one. He let the top of the picture cut off the sky just above the mountain peaks; the bottom side cut off the water just below Anna's boots. He always designed the composition of his photographs in the viewfinder. Composition was a far too important part of photography to be left in the hands of the picture editor or lay-out team.

He shot about twenty frames, some with a slightly smaller aperture, some with a slightly greater, just to be sure of the exposure. Then he bent down to the water with the camera and transformed the idyll into a drama, by placing the whirling water in the foreground. The wide-angle lens was a perfect instrument for manipulating reality. He finished the film.

He had barely put in the new roll when Haseke shouted from where he stood in the water by the upper part of the Cove.

'I've got one!'

Ken hurried along the semi-circular shoreline to the lower rock. He switched over to the camera with the telephoto lens.

Haseke's glittering line pointed to the spot where the fish was. Trembling, it wandered out into the mainstream. The line went slack. Suddenly, there was the fish. Ken followed its jump through the viewfinder. Down it splashed. He had not pressed the shutter. The fish was too far out in the stream.

The sparkling line wandered in towards the Cove. He had it in the centre of the lens. Haseke entered the picture. The fish jumped in a spraying arc. He pressed the shutter.

Bull's eye.

The fisherman and the fish in the same picture.

He checked the distance. Fifteen metres. Perfect. With the aperture he had used, the depth of field extended from six metres to infinity.

He climbed down from the rock and followed the shore to keep a straight line to the fish and Haseke. The fish went into the Cove. It jumped again. But this time outside the picture.

'It won't jump again,' said the major, who had gone up on land with Anna. 'Three times is the maximum.'

'I must have more jumps,' said Ken.

He knew he was about to take the perfect photograph of a fish. Perhaps he already had. The picture he had taken was a bull's eye, there was no doubt about it, but he needed three bull's eyes to be completely sure.

'What a kick,' he said to Anna. 'Did you see when it jumped and the water sprayed in the direct light? Everything was perfect. What a kick!'

Haseke reeled in the salmon trout, unhooked it and released it into the water. The major and Anna resumed their places. Ken devoted ten minutes to them, until Haseke was again busy with a trout.

During the next three hours Haseke caught six trout, which altogether made a total of ten good jumps above the surface. Ken was sure that he had taken five shots with Haseke in the picture. At least three were bull's eyes. Ken was satisfied.

So was Haseke. He was brimming over with enthusiasm as he weighed the fish, and he obviously found it difficult to subdue his delight to suit the sombre atmosphere which the death had cast over the day. The major was pleased too. He nodded to Ken with that knowing air of players in a winning team: now we are sure of victory.

Peter Baxter had appeared during the photographing and, while working, Ken had noticed the major taking Peter aside and telling him what had happened. He had also noticed the major asking Peter to go up to the kitchen for some beer. Peter was just the type of person that someone like the major would bully.

While the major gathered dry willow twigs and began to build a bonfire, Ken took close-up shots: small still lifes of the rod and reel, of the fly and the fish's mouth, of the flybox and fish and of all the different combinations of these ingredients. Then the major asked if he could have the fish; he wanted to lay them on the fire and organize a simple beach party.

Soon the three largest trout were wrapped in foil and put on to the fire. The group settled down on the grass and on the rocks and drank beer, waiting for the trout to cook. The bonfire crackled and blazed pleasantly.

'This is happiness,' said Haseke. 'Modern man is happiest when he gets back to his primitive origins. A blazing fire in the open air, food and drink in the company of friends, all this after having satisfied his hunting instinct; even Neanderthal man must have experienced this as the greatest joy in life.'

'I haven't satisfied any hunting instinct,' said Anna. 'And I'm enjoying myself anyway.'

'I'm speaking about us men,' said Haseke. 'We're the ones who have a hunting instinct, not you women. We're the ones who enjoy hunting and fishing, not you. We've inherited this from Neanderthal man. The bag and catch were the very object of a man's existence, but for a woman they were merely the raw materials for her life's work: the preparation of food and clothing.'

It was twilight and the sun was setting. It had already deserted the river valley and drew itself farther and farther up the mountain slope. It was already so late in the year that the sun stayed below the horizon for several hours around midnight. This suited Ken well. The Midnight Sun might well be an excellent tourist attraction, but he had never understood the appeal of the sun shining day and night like the constant glaring light in an isolation cell.

The major poked out one of the foil packets with a stick and opened it carefully in order not to burn his fingers. The pink flesh loosened easily from the backbone.

'Ready,' said the major, and raked the other two packets out of the coals.

'Let us now taste this fish which died for our sake,' said Ken.

'Wunderbar,' pronounced Fräulein Krämer, whose mouth was the same light pink colour as the fish she'd just chewed.

'We'll be sure to use this in the advertising campaign,' said Haseke. 'Europe's over-civilized multitudes just need to be informed that something like this exists and they'll do anything to come here. To catch their own fish, cook it over an open fire, eat with their fingers, and maybe even sleep out of doors one night, that's something they've never done in the whole of their lives.'

'It can be arranged,' said the major.

'Personally, I prefer a comfortable bed,' said Anna. 'And someone to make it for me in the morning. Oh, I'm sorry,' she said, when she realized that her remark could be taken as a complaint about having to make her own bed that morning. 'Naturally I wasn't referring to this morning.'

'Surely your bed was made this morning?' said the major.

'No,' said Anna. 'But it doesn't matter. I didn't mean it like that.'

'My bed wasn't made either,' said Ken.

'In our room the beds were made and everything was tidied,' said Haseke.

'Mine too,' said the major.

'But mine wasn't,' said Peter Baxter.

'Peculiar,' said Anna.

'It looks as if we might have a thunderstorm,' said the major. Ken looked at the horizon in the west where dark, threatening thunderclouds were gathering. A faint rumbling dispelled any uncertainty about the question.

'Festivities were broken off on account of the imminent storm,' he said.

'It'll take a while before it reaches us,' said the major.

Ken took his cameras out of the bag and began taking pictures of the people sitting around the bonfire by the river, surrounded by mountains.

'Peculiar,' repeated Anna. 'It's strange that the housekeeper hadn't finished making the beds. Obviously she cleaned the rooms in order, beginning at the entrance. She'd finished tidying two rooms before she was interrupted. Who's living in the third room? Something must have happened there that made her go down to the river.'

'The Danes are staying in that room,' said the major. 'But they hadn't seen her. Or so they said.'

'Where are they now? Why aren't they here?'

'They're probably in their room,' said the major.

'I think it's peculiar,' said Anna. 'The Danes are the only ones who could have seen the housekeeper from the place where they were posted this morning. The Table Rock is the only pool which has a clear view of the lodge. That's where the Danes were. And now it turns out that the housekeeper interrupted her bedmaking in their room.'

'Don't get all excited, Anna,' said Ken. 'You're taking an ordinary accident and blowing it up into a thrilling detective mystery. You magazine writers are always true to type. Come here instead, and put a piece of salmon in your mouth. That's right. Don't look as if you regretted its dying for your sake. Smile a little. A little more. Good. Your hair looks lovely against the mountains.'

He took one picture after another while he was talking. Anna followed his instructions obediently.

'Good girl,' he said when he'd finished the roll.

'Exactly what was the matter with the radio?' asked Anna. 'Isn't it odd that it broke down just when it was most needed?'

'I don't know what went wrong,' said the major. 'In the army we don't use radios with printed circuits. We only trust the ones with bulbs and tubes.'

'But I've had experience with short-wave radios,' said Peter. 'You should have fetched me to have a look at the instrument. It's an ordinary System 70, isn't it?'

'Can't you have a look at it now?' asked Anna. "Maybe you can get it to work.'

'It's in Grahn's room,' said the major. 'Go through the kitchen. Grahn's room is on the far left.'

Peter stood up. He hesitated for a while. Then he began to walk up the slope. Obedient as always, thought Ken.

Ken had considered taking some photos of Fräulein Krämer. But could not get over her make-up. The girl was completely retouched. He wondered why heavily painted women always seemed cheap. Perhaps it was because they looked as if they painted themselves for the benefit of the gallery and not for the stalls.

Fräulein Krämer did not seem to be enjoying herself. She had only said one word during the entire meal and had probably understood even less. Suddenly Haseke noticed her, helped her to her feet and began to walk along the shore with her. Ken thought it looked as if he were walking a dog.

'Those two Danes, who are they exactly?' Anna asked the major. 'They seem strange to me and those heavy bags they brought... very queer.'

'They're travel consultants,' said the major. 'They represent Tjäreborg Tours. One of Tjäreborg's directors rang us up and asked if he could send two of his people as observers. Naturally, we didn't say no. And so, these two gentlemen arrived on the train.'

'On the train! That's the strangest thing of all. Surely you agree? Why would two Tjäreborg representatives travel all the way from Copenhagen and right through Sweden by train?'

Peter came walking down the slope. There was a kind of vigour in his walk as if he were a scout on his first important mission. Anna and the major got up. Ken remained seated.

'It's no wonder the radio is useless,' said Peter, when he'd arrived.

'Why's that?' asked the major.

'One of the couplings has been removed.'

'What the hell does that mean?' The major raised his voice.

'It can only mean one thing: sabotage.'

A rumble came from the dark clouds in the east. Lightning flashed. The storm came nearer.

9

ANNA'S EYES FOLLOWED the major climbing the slope with Peter in tow. A resolute man with a powerful stride and determined jaw. She hated being left out when something important was happening. And what was happening now had been set off by her. She was the one who had raised the suspicions about the Danes and drawn the conclusion that all was not as it should be. Now, when the Danes were about to be driven into a corner, she was not allowed to come along. She hated the major's superior attitude: we'll take care of this, little lady. And this Peter. How could *he* be of any help? He was as useless as a burnt-out candle in the dark.

'Take it easy, baby,' said Ken. 'Stay here with me by the bonfire. Haven't you noticed we have company? The mosquitoes have started appearing.'

'Don't you baby me!'

'Now begins the first skirmish in the great battle with the mosquitoes, the tireless defenders of the wilderness.'

'But this is really suspicious.'

'There's always a cloud in the sky in Norrland,' continued Ken. 'A cloud of mosquitoes.'

'What's the matter with you? Aren't you interested in how this all fits together?'

'Kitten,' laughed Ken. 'Don't be too curious. You'll burn your paws and singe your whiskers.'

Anna dug her fingernails into her palm. Long pointed nails were all she had in common with a woman like Fräulein Krämer. But even Anna needed this excessive feminine equipment. To help control herself when men treated her in the usual manner: as an irresponsible child. Or even worse: as an irresponsible animal. She refused to let herself be treated as if she were endowed with whiskers and paws, even if it was well meant. Especially if it was well meant.

'Excuse me,' she said, as calmly as she could, and turning her back on Ken, she began to walk up the hill. Both men ahead of her had already disappeared over the top of the hill, which concealed the cottages from this part of the river. She quickened her pace. A flash of lightning lit up the dark clouds which were still gathering. The thunder sounded like a cannon shot. The storm was very near.

Ken had called her curious. That was not how she saw herself. She was not curious. She was a person who sought the answers to questions. Partly it was her nature, and partly it was her job. She saw life as something about which she needed to learn as much as possible, as a series of endless connections to be made. She used to say that she was a radical in the original meaning of the word. The word radical came from radix, the Latin word for root. She always wanted to get to the root of things.

While walking up the path to the top of the hill, she noticed that Ken was right about the mosquitoes. They had suddenly appeared from nowhere, and were swarming around her in their thousands. A few had already settled on her skin to slake their thirst for blood. Their drone grated on her ears.

When she reached the top, neither of the men was to be seen.

They must have reached the building. Probably they had already started talking with the Danes. But when she came into the yard, there was no sound of the heated conversation she was expecting. Even the corridor was completely silent when she opened the door to the guest cottage and entered.

The door to the Danes' room stood ajar. She peeped in. The major and Peter were in there alone. They were searching the room as if they were two thieves hunting for hidden diamonds.

'What are you doing?' she asked.

'The two heavy bags are missing,' said the major. 'So are the Danes. We're searching. Maybe we'll find a clue to what they're up to. We need someone to keep watch, so that we aren't taken by surprise.'

Anna went back to the outer door and stood by the steps. The storm clouds were directly overhead, so the rain could not be far away. There was no sign of anyone.

She heard voices from the Danes' room and gathered that something had happened. She ran quickly to have a look. Peter held a bunch of yellow flexes in each hand.

'Have you ever seen these before?' The major was upset. 'They're electric detonators. They detonate instantly with no delayed action. You can tell by the yellow colour. Jesus! Where did you find them?'

'Stuffed into a sock in the bottom of the luggage.'

'I can't believe it. It's pure sabotage equipment. These detonators are used to set off gelignite. You put them into the gelignite, connect them to a battery and switch on the current. It explodes instantly. What the hell do they have them for?'

'Perhaps there is gelignite in those bags they've taken away. Maybe these detonators are meant for that,' said Anna.

'Don't stand here!' said the major. 'Go back and keep watch. They could return any time.'

Anna repositioned herself on the steps to the entrance. There was still no sign of anyone. The thunderclouds covered the valley like a blanket. It had grown as dark as night. She was confused. The housekeeper's death, the sabotaged radio, the detonators—her thoughts got stuck there, circling round and round and always returning to the same starting point.

Suddenly she spotted the two Danes approaching from behind the main building. She ran into the corridor and shouted.

'They're coming!'

The major and Peter came out of the door. The major locked it quickly and hung the key on the hook outside the next room. Anna followed them when they went towards the door. She did not want to be left alone in the guest cottage with the two Danes.

They ran into them on the steps. Steiner smiled as usual; Moll nodded severely when they greeted each other. No one said a word. Steiner and Moll continued into their room; the major and Peter crossed the yard to the main building. Anna followed.

When they entered Grahn's room, Anna stayed outside in the kitchen. She heard the major urge Peter to hurry up. They had to get the radio working so that they could alert the police in Kiruna. Then the door shut.

Anna lit the gas cooker and put on a kettle of water to boil. She would decide later what to use it for. For the moment it provided a feeling of purpose for her presence in the kitchen.

Suddenly there was a bang as if a lorry full of scrap iron had fallen from the sky. A tremendous noise came from the other building, and a door slammed open.

Running footsteps in the corridor. The outer door flung open. Steiner and Moll came dashing across the yard and into the main building. The floorboards boomed in the dining room. Now they were in the kitchen, Steiner first. He stopped in front of Grahn's door and prevented Moll from tugging it open.

Slowly Steiner opened the door. Anna saw the major turn. Peter sat at a table busy with a screwdriver and a radio transmitter.

'What in hell's name are you doing?' The major's face was red with anger. 'Who gave you permission to barge in here?'

'We're only following your example, major,' said Steiner. 'You've just broken into our room. Now we're breaking into yours.'

'Get out!'

'You took something that belongs to us. We want it back.'

'Out, I said!'

The major stood up and went directly towards Steiner.

'Out!'

Steiner took one step aside and let Moll come forward. It

seemed to Anna like a well-practised move in a game. When the major reached the doorway, it was not little Steiner, but huge Moll, who faced him. He reached out his hands to show Moll out of the room. Moll grabbed his fingers and bent them backwards. The major screamed with pain and was forced down onto his knees.

Moll rammed his knee into the major's chin. Hard. The jolt threw the major backwards. He hit the floor with a crash, which spread through the planks and made Anna's legs vibrate, then lay on his back with his arms extended and mouth gaping.

Anna did not move. She had never seen real violence before. Moll's assault on the major made her feel sick. For a moment she could hardly see. She grasped the sink to keep her balance.

Moll went over to the major, searched his pockets and pulled out the two bunches of electric detonators. The major rolled over on to his side and tried to get up on all fours.

'Help the old soldier on to the bed,' said Steiner, nodding to Peter, who was still sitting at the table with the screwdriver in his hand. 'I'm sure he needs to recover.'

Peter did not move. He just stared at the major, who feebly attempted to get up on to his knees.

Suddenly a wave of passion surged through Anna. She stepped right up to Steiner. She couldn't control herself.

'How disgusting!' she said. 'How disgusting you are! How thoroughly disgusting!'

'Oh,' said Steiner. 'That was nothing. You should see us when we really get going.'

'Hey, you, in the kitchen!' came a voice from the dining room which Anna immediately recognized. It was Ken. Footsteps approached, and Ken entered the kitchen. 'What the hell are you doing?'

He stopped.

'Whoops!' he exclaimed. 'Is it real?'

He was staring at an object in Steiner's hand. It was a pistol. A black pistol with a long barrel. Anna had never seen a real pistol before, but this one was real without a doubt.

Haseke emerged from behind Ken's back, followed by a blonde streak of hair, Fräulein Krämer.

'Ladies and gentlemen,' said Steiner. 'I have an announcement to make to you!'

He paused long enough to grin. Then he said slowly: 'You can consider yourselves hostages.'

10

A<small>NNA WAS SHOCKED</small>. At the same time she was unmoved. She was shocked in the biological sense: her mouth was dry, her hands trembled, her legs felt shaky, her stomach was knotted. But intellectually she was unmoved. She could not believe that this was real; that this was actually happening now and not in a nightmare.

Maybe it was an occupational hazard. Dramatic occurrences happened to other people; she only appeared after the fact to interview the people involved and write about them. People survived plane crashes, gave birth to deformed children, were betrayed after thirty years of marriage, were raped, robbed, assaulted or won the grand prize in a lottery. The world was a play and she was its critic.

You can consider yourselves hostages, Steiner had said. Then he and Moll had shown the others into the dining room. They had sat down around the same table as during Grahn's runthrough of the pools that morning. Steiner stood where Grahn had been. Moll sat down next to him in a Windsor chair. He sat there with his arms crossed, his thick thighs spread a little apart, and his heavy head resting like a stone on his shoulders.

The storm was right over them now. The thunder boomed like a sound-effect in a television programme about World War II; the rain pattered on the window panes as if someone were shooting peas at them through a blow-pipe.

'I understand your surprise,' said Steiner. 'You've naturally never been hostages before. And certainly you're also confused. What is this, you're wondering. Isn't this something that happens to aeroplanes and ambassadors? Certainly it is. But we're just a bit more original. We've seized a fishing lodge in the wilderness.'

Steiner spoke calmly and normally, as if he were giving a lecture. But to avoid any misunderstanding, he had placed the pistol on the table in front of him as a reminder that he was capable of dealing with any disturbances in the audience.

'What will become of us, you're wondering,' he continued. 'Ladies and gentlemen, don't worry. Nothing will happen to you. That is, if you do as you're told. And we require so little. Just that you stay calm. Don't make trouble. Don't attempt anything foolish.'

Anna looked at the others while Steiner was speaking. The major sat with his hand holding his jaw where Moll's knee had struck it. Haseke had his arm around Fräulein Krämer's shoulders. Her eye make-up had smudged on to her cheeks. Peter stared straight forward with a dull look, the same hopeless look one sees among old-age pensioners. Ken was the same as ever; he did not seem to take anything seriously.

'As I said,' continued Steiner, 'if you don't attempt anything foolish, you've got nothing to fear. Simply carry on as usual. Go to bed tonight and in the morning, start fishing again. Your movements will have to be temporarily restricted. You must stay at one pool, the Table Rock. It can be seen from here and I don't want anyone going out of sight. Naturally, no one must leave. Neither tonight nor tomorrow. It's not worth trying. Imagine you're imprisoned in a concentration camp. Nature's own concentration camp. The mountains are the walls. The great distance is the barbed wire. And to make the barbs extra sharp, Moll is about to collect your shoes.'

'What exactly is the point of all this?' asked the major. 'We demand to know what you're after!'

Steiner took a cigar out of his inner pocket and lit it with a match. He took a deep puff and exhaled the smoke up towards the ceiling.

'Is it really too much to ask you to tell us why you've taken us hostage?' This again from the major.

'You're beginning to get tiresome, Major.' Steiner drew his hand through his hair nervously. 'You're speaking out of turn. You've no more self-discipline than a spoiled schoolgirl.'

The major grasped the edge of the table and raised himself halfway as if he planned to attack Steiner. Moll uncrossed his arms. That had the same effect as if he had drawn a weapon. The major sank back into his seat. Moll crossed his arms again, and sat motionless. Now and again he flared his nostrils like the bloodhound he really was.

Steiner smiled.

'Of course, you wonder why you've been taken hostage,' he said. 'You ask yourselves, what do they want from us? Ladies and gentlemen, you shall have the answer to your question. We don't want anything from you. All we want is peace and quiet. We've sought out this spot in the wilderness to be in peace. But do we get it? No! There are those among you, ladies and gentlemen, who break into our room, search through our luggage and steal our possessions. We can't tolerate this. We don't want to be treated like this, Moll and I said to each other. We must do something to get our peace. We'll take them hostage.'

'Nonsense,' said the major. 'First of all, you sabotaged the radio. Then you have detonators in your luggage. What do you have them for? And what was in those bags? I'm sure it was gelignite. I'd like to know what you're planning to use it for!'

Steiner stuck his hand in his pocket and drew out an object which he held between his thumb and index finger. Anna thought it looked like an electric contact switch.

'I just borrowed this piece,' said Steiner. 'I knew you planned to use the radio to call the police from Kiruna. What a fuss that would have been. And only for a housekeeper who went and tumbled into the river. Naturally, I wanted to prevent that!'

Anna's sense of unreality continued. She was experiencing the scene in the dining room as if, at any moment, the director might rush out from backstage and stop the play, praise Steiner for his light tone and the major for his vivid insight. Suddenly it occurred to her that she ought to take notes, record dialogue, gestures and moods. Even though she herself had a part in this play, she was still the critic. She was in the midst of sensational material for an article.

'There were explosives,' said the major. 'Explosives and detonators. I demand an answer to my question.'

'You can demand whatever you like, Major. I don't give a

damn. We're here to carry out a mission, not to answer questions. We won't allow anyone to stop us. Especially not a discharged officer.'

'You've forgotten one thing,' said the major. 'By now Grahn has certainly reached the fishing lodge farther down the river. He'll have contacted the police in Kiruna from there with the radio. We can expect them here any time now.'

'The trouble with you, Major, is that you still haven't understood what's happened,' said Steiner. 'You think you've fallen into the hands of a couple of crazy criminals who are subjecting you to pointless persecution. That's not the case. We're professionals with long experience. Anyone who's waiting for Grahn to reach somewhere and to alert the police, is waiting in vain. You can't expect anything from that man ever again.'

He snapped his fingers and Moll stuck his hand in his pocket, pulled out a sheath knife and threw it on the table in front of Steiner. It was a beautifully decorated Lapp knife, the same knife Anna had seen hanging from Grahn's belt.

Anna felt a wave of faintness swell over her. This was violence demonstrated in the most devastating way possible. That Grahn was dead was just as clear as if they had shown his name on a gravestone.

11

OUT IN THE yard the rain poured down over them and they ran for cover under the roof of the guest cottage. They stood inside the door and stared at each other, soaking wet and confused, like demonstrators, who had been sprayed by fire-hoses.

'We must have a meeting,' said the major after a while.

'First of all, we need to change and dry off a bit,' said Haseke. He held Sabine firmly around the shoulders and led her to their bedroom. Anna noticed how Sabine's wet hair clung to her head and how her wet clothes drooped on her body.

'Let's say we'll meet in my room in half an hour,' said the major.

'In an hour,' said Haseke as he entered the room and closed the door behind Sabine and himself.

'All right, agreed,' said the major and continued saying something else to which Anna did not have the strength to listen. She went down the corridor to her room, opened the door and entered.

One of the wardrobe doors stood open and in the mirror on its inside she could see herself full length, a darker and more substantial version of Sabine, just as wet, just as drooping, just as pathetic. She looked down at the soaking wet socks on her feet. Moll had taken away her shoes.

Steiner and Moll had finished off the meeting in the main building by searching everyone. Moll had confiscated Haseke's and the major's sheath knives and Peter Baxter's clasp knife. Then he had gone to search their bedrooms. He returned with a paper bag half full of shoes. Steiner ordered everyone to take off the shoes they had on, and Moll stuffed these into the bag as well. No one made any objections.

Finally, Steiner sent Moll over to the guest cottage again, this time to fetch their own personal luggage. He explained that he and Moll planned to stay in Grahn's room. The entire main building was forbidden territory from now on. No one was allowed to set foot in there until the following morning when the major had his radio hook-up. When Moll returned, Steiner bowed with exaggerated courtesy and bade them all good night.

Anna shut the wardrobe door with its mirror but remained standing and staring blankly at the black door handle. The rain beat against a window pane far away in another reality. She stood frozen. Frozen to her marrow. She thought about the housekeeper's death and about Grahn's. She thought about the two who had murdered them, Steiner and Moll. What did they have planned for the rest of them? What did they have planned for her? She felt alone. Afraid and alone.

There was a knock at the door.

Anna gave a start.

'Who is it?'

'Ken.'

She opened the door and Ken walked into the room. He had

changed into dry jeans and a blue jersey. In one hand he held a bottle. Without giving her a chance to stop him, he walked past her, went over to the table and filled two glasses that stood there.

'Whisky,' he said. 'I thought you'd need something to warm you up.'

He came towards her with the glass. He stopped suddenly as if he'd just seen her. His smile faded.

'Jesus!' he said. 'You haven't changed your clothes yet.'

'What do you think is going to happen to us?'

'Anna, listen!' Ken stood in front of her. 'You must pull yourself together! It's no use your standing here soaking wet and freezing. Here!' He offered her the glass. 'Drink this! Then go and change!'

She took the glass and took a big swig. The whisky was so strong that she could feel it burn its way down her throat into her stomach. She took another gulp.

'Do you think they're going to kill us?' she said.

'The greatest danger threatening you right now is that you'll catch pneumonia from standing here soaking wet.'

'Yes.' Anna emptied the glass. 'They killed the housekeeper and Grahn,' she added.

Ken took her by the shoulders and shook her warily as if he was trying to wake her.

'You must take off your wet clothes,' he said.

Anna felt his hand unbuttoning the top button of her shirt and then one button after another, until the shirt was completely open in front. She did not react. It was as if this undressing were happening to a strange woman, not to her. She did not react until Ken took the shirt off her shoulders and exposed her breasts. Then she pushed aside his hand and went into the bathroom.

She took off her shirt, jeans, pants and socks, everything she had had on. She dried her body with a large white bath towel, then her hair. She looked at herself in the bathroom mirror. She looked at her breasts. They were round and full, with nipples that grew large and smooth after having been shrivelled.

She wondered what Ken had thought of them. Men were usually turned on by all female breasts within reasonable limits; she knew this because breasts were one of the most important points of sale in publishing. But Ken was an exception. Female breasts had been his speciality during his stint as a pin-up photographer. Maybe he was satiated. She held her hands under her breasts and weighed them slowly. She thought about Ken's hands, tanned, strong, safe.

She began to comb her hair. As usual she did this carefully, so that she got it the way she wanted it. So that it formed a dark frame around her face which she knew suited her. She could, of course, analyse her behaviour. She knew full well that she was yielding to a biological urge to appear attractive to a prospective mate of the opposite sex. She also knew that this intellectual analysis stood no chance of overcoming the pleasant feeling of warmth which spread through her as she thought about the man in the next room.

She remembered a debate in the women's group at her college of journalism. Someone had begun discussing the fact that more children are born in wartime than in peacetime. Someone else had come up with an explanation: when a woman is lonely and afraid she always reaches for a penis just as a drowning man catches at a straw. They had all laughed. They were all happy and strong. None of them lonely or afraid.

The memory of the day's terrible occurrences came back to her. She took a deep breath, put a strand of hair in place, wrapped herself in a dressing gown and went out to Ken.

'Good girl.' Ken stood with a glass ready in his hand. 'Drink this and you'll feel even better.'

She took the glass.

'Thanks,' she said.

'You're shivering,' he said.

She looked down at the whisky sloshing uneasily in the glass she held in her hand.

'Yes,' she said. 'I'm rather upset.'

She emptied the glass and held it out to Ken. Then she took a step towards him and let her arms fall to her sides with the typically female pose that implied she didn't want to take the initiative herself, but at the same time that she would consider it a personal insult if the man did not.

Ken put the glass on the table. For an instant he stood in front of Anna and looked her straight in the eye. She met his glance. Without a word, they came to the same agreement as men and women have done throughout the ages, to set aside all antagonism and all differences. All except one: the difference in sex.

Ken put his hands on her shoulders, drew her towards him and held her tight. Anna felt the tension in her body relax as when she had been a tired little girl and had just crept in under the covers.

She put her hands under his jersey and stroked his back up towards his shoulders and felt in her palms the warmth of his body and the strength of his muscles.

Slowly Ken let go of her, opened her dressing gown, took it off her shoulders and let it fall to the floor. He took her breasts gently and held them in his hands. She took hold of his jersey, pulled it off, pressed her breasts against his bare skin and was filled with wonder that she did not more often allow her anxiety and loneliness to dissolve and melt away in the warmth of another human body.

For an instant they stood still next to each other with their arms around each others waists. Then one of his hands found her breast again and held it tight. Her heart beat underneath his hand and filled her limbs with an endless sweetness. Her hips surged forward towards him. She felt the hard pressure of his penis against her belly. Her hands came to life, moved to his belt and started unfastening the buckle.

Ken took over. He pulled off his trousers and came up to her again. She took hold of his penis in her hand. If this was a woman's last straw, she thought, it must be the strongest straw in the world.

She stood on her toes, spread open her thighs, and took him into her as passionately as if her whole life had been aiming towards this moment. She did something that she had never done before. She gave herself to a near stranger. As completely as if it were the last action in her life.

12

Sabine's sobbing let up and became the even breathing of sleep—rhythmic, like swells washing up on the shore. Haseke sat on the bed next to her and saw the light from the bedside lamp glinting on her blonde hair and on the down of her tanned arm. He had taken her into their bedroom, given her a powerful sleeping pill and put her to bed like a child.

Fear was not to be shown in public, he felt. In private one could be as afraid as one liked. But perhaps this rule applied only to men. Sabine had not been the least bit ashamed to show that she was terrified. Nevertheless, he had taken care of her and isolated her from the others as if she suffered from some shameful disease.

She had clung to him as if she sought the security of her father's arms. He sighed. If it was the need for security that made her accept his attentions, then he had truly failed her by involving her in this affair. He had met her at a party two months ago. An ordinary Lufthansa air hostess, who had chosen her career believing that truly rewarding relationships were established in the sky.

He saw her young body attractively outlined under the cover. He did not feel like her father any longer. He felt like her grandfather. It occurred to him that he was using her as King David had used Abisag, the young woman laid next to him to warm his body when he was dying.

He turned towards the mirror over the night table and looked at his face, his unavoidable companion who suited him less and less each year. What was he doing with such an old companion?

Now. The comedy was over now. He had recognized Steiner and Moll. He had learned to recognize these henchmen of death from the difficult time in Germany during Hitler's rule. He had lived among them. These sure men with cold hearts and looks without compassion. Who justified their actions by making them their duty. Who took away men in the night and crushed their limbs. Who shot women and children. Who did their duty. This was the anatomy of evil. Evil exerts itself by dividing its resolution and execution between different people. The person who decides to commit an atrocity never needs to carry it out. He never taints his hands, never has to see the suffering for which he is responsible. On the other hand, the person who carries out the deed, feels no responsibility for it. He is merely doing his duty.

He had recognized them again as soon as they went into action. He had recognized them by the way they treated people as objects, by the way in which they dismissed murder. He had understood that these men were professional killers. They had no compassion for their victims. They did not plan to let anyone survive. Reprieve was a completely unknown concept to them. They had postponed the execution merely for practical reasons.

He got up from Sabine's bed and went out of the room. The others had agreed to meet in the major's room to discuss the situation. He knocked on the door and entered.

'Madmen,' said the major. 'We've fallen into the hands of two madmen.'

The room had the air of conspiracy: the dim lighting, the thick cigarette smoke, the tense looks on the faces of those present. The major, Anna and Ken sat on chairs around the table by the window. Peter Baxter sat on the bed, leaning against the wall.

'Madmen,' repeated the major. He took the whisky bottle which stood on the table, filled the empty glass remaining and offered it Haseke.

'No,' said Haseke. 'They aren't madmen. That's exactly what they're pretending to be. They're two professional criminals on a mission.'

He took the glass and tasted the whisky. The major filled up his own glass and toasted the others. Then he drew a chair up to the table and Haseke sat down. A flash of lightning lit up the world outside the window. The landscape was flooded with rain.

'Nonsense,' said the major. 'What kind of mission could they have up here? There's nothing here except us.'

'Maybe they're secret agents for Spies Travel Agency,' said Ken. 'Disguised as Tjäreborg Agency consultants; I think that would be funny. Mission: the enemy establishment in northern Sweden. Investigate and disrupt. Competition is tough between travel agencies nowadays.'

'Are there any top-secret defence structures near here?' Haseke turned to the major. 'You should know—you were in the army.'

'Yes, I was,' said the major. 'But there's nothing like that around here. Nothing at all. Just us. Seizing a tourist resort, it's madness!'

'But there's method in the madness,' said Haseke. 'They have explosives and detonators with them. In suitcases which they've dragged all the way from Denmark or wherever they come from. By the way, how did they get to Kiruna? They couldn't have flown. Not with pistols. Security at airports is far too strict nowadays. Not with explosives either.'

'They came by train,' said the major. 'I met them myself at the railway station. I thought it was peculiar that they didn't arrive by plane. Now I understand why.'

'From the start they'd already planned to blast something up here,' continued Haseke. 'What? I'd guess it was this dam here above us.'

'That's a thought,' said the major. 'Power stations and dams were main targets during the war.'

'Wake up, Major,' said Ken. 'The war's over now. Power stations in Sweden today are completely without interest as targets for sabotage. What exactly is on your mind? Do you think it's an attack by the international oil companies? Do you think they want to disrupt the production of electricity in Sweden in order to sell us more oil?'

'Gelignite,' said the major. 'It fits in with the gelignite. I mean, if I were planning to blast this dam, I'd use gelignite. And gelignite is obviously what they've got with them in that bag. The detonators we found in their room are typical. Gelignite is ideal for blasting a dam. It's malleable and has an adhesive quality like plasticine. You stick a few kilos of the stuff at the foundation of each gate. Then you put in the detonators, connect them to a battery and send off the electrical impulse. The gates open immediately.'

'You can bury yourself in the technique of explosives as much as you like,' said Ken. 'But that still doesn't prove that they were planning to blow up this dam.'

'Let me see,' continued the major. 'The dam has two gates. That means four foundations. Let's assume that you use five kilos per foundation—that should suffice. That makes twenty kilos altogether. And a little extra. That's a heavy load. Especially if you add electrical wires, batteries, pistols and ammunition. It's understandable that the bags were so heavy.'

'But why?' asked Ken patiently. 'You still haven't explained why they'd want to blow up the dam.'

'Not the foundations, in fact.' The major wouldn't abandon his line of thought. 'One ought to blow up the opening device, that would be more effective, it must be the weakest point. But it doesn't change the technique.'

'The main purpose doesn't necessarily have to be destroying the dam itself,' said Haseke.

'Exactly,' said Ken. 'Anyone could get bored with all this fuss with spinners and flies. Set off an explosion so that something really exciting happens.'

Haseke attributed Ken's peculiar joke to grim humour. People reacted differently when their lives were threatened. Sabine had collapsed, Peter Baxter seemed crippled where he sat on the bed, the major drank one glass of whisky after another, Ken joked. Only Anna seemed normal, calm and blossoming, enclosed in a feminine security which was sufficient unto itself. He himself felt calm and secure. His consciousness was alert. He knew that his ability to function well in critical situations was one of his best qualities.

'The main purpose may be to destroy something lying below the dam,' he said. 'If millions of cubic metres of water are let loose at once, an incredible force will be released. It'll create a flood which will sweep with it everything in the valley. Including us. We don't stand a chance of surviving.'

'I just don't understand what good it would do,' said Ken. 'Why would they go to so much trouble to drown us when they could shoot us right on the spot if they wanted?'

'You're forgetting that there's another lodge further downstream. Suppose it's that lodge which is the Danes' target. In that case, we have a logical explanation for everything that's happened. Including the housekeeper's death and Grahn's. All the puzzle pieces fit together. The pattern is complete.'

'I don't understand.' The major refilled his glass.

'Let me begin with the housekeeper's death,' said Haseke. 'Something occurred while she was cleaning our bedrooms. We know that all the rooms before the Danes' were already tidied, whereas the other rooms were untouched. The conclusion is obvious: she must have been interrupted in the Danes' room. My guess is that she found something which made her suspect that all wasn't well.'

'She'd said that from the start,' said the major. 'She told me that the Danes had ordered her to stay out of their room. They wanted to take care of it themselves. She didn't approve of that. She said that she wouldn't stand for it. I'm sure she entered the room and took a good look around. Maybe she found the explosives in their bags. It's true the bags weren't there when we found the detonators, but they must have been there in the morning.'

'But why did they leave the detonators behind?' asked Anna.

'You don't drag detonators around unnecessarily. They're dangerous; they could easily blow off a hand if they went off by accident. But most of all, they're sensitive to moisture. The gelignite, however, can be handled without worry. I'm sure it's hidden somewhere near the dam.'

'Let's suppose then that she found the explosives,' said Haseke. 'And the Danes discovered this. Probably they had the guest cottage under watch at all times. They knew that the morning was the most vulnerable time; that's to say the time before they had the opportunity to carry off the explosives and hide them somewhere. Their secret was exposed by the housekeeper. There was only one thing to do: silence the housekeeper forever. They could never explain away thirty kilos of explosives. That's why the housekeeper was killed. Whether it happened in their room, or whether she was alive when she was thrown into the river, I can't say. Everyone was at their pool. No one would have seen the Danes carrying her down to the Table Rock where they were posted. One thing, however, is clear. Her death was not an accidental drowning. She was murdered.'

'Now I see why they were eager to be placed at the Table Rock,' said the major.

'It was, of course, their bad luck that the housekeeper discovered them,' continued Haseke. 'Ideally they would have worked quietly and let the explosion come as a surprise for the rest of us. That must have been their plan at the start. The situation changed. They must at all costs prevent the housekeeper's death from causing someone to contact the police. That's why they tried to make it look as if she'd drowned. That's why they sabotaged the radio. That's why Moll went after Grahn and killed him as well. And that's why we've been taken hostage, as they call it. We must be held in check until their mission is completed, and the dam is blasted.'

'But what are they after?' asked Anna. 'What's at the other lodge? What kind of lodge is it?'

'I only know what Grahn told me before he left,' said the major. 'The lodge belongs to the National Board of Crown Forests and Lands. They use it for entertainment purposes. Political big shots go there to fish. They have complete peace from the press and curious people. Finland's president has been there many times. The King as well.'

Suddenly he banged his fist on the table.

'Wait,' he cried. 'What was it Grahn said? Yes, there's a guest coming from England tomorrow evening. A very important guest. His stay is surrounded with great secrecy.'

'How do you know it's an Englishman, then?' asked Anna.

'Grahn had spoken to the warden of the lodge, who's a good friend of his. He was in Kiruna brushing up on his English.'

'Technically, he could also be an American, then,' said Haseke. 'Even Americans speak English.'

'American,' said Anna thoughtfully.

'He could be any nationality in that case,' said Ken. 'Everyone speaks English, even if they come from Nigeria.'

'I think,' said Anna, 'I know who it is.'

The room grew silent. The rain beat against the window panes. Everyone stared at Anna.

'It all fits,' she continued. 'Important person. American. Assassination attempts. Besides, I know he was going fishing somewhere in Sweden.'

'Who is it?' asked the major. 'Tell us who it is!'

'Stockwell,' said Anna. 'The American peace-senator.'

13

'IT'S TRUE HE didn't actually say he was going fishing,' concluded Anna. 'But he said it in a roundabout way. "Don't think I'm out chasing girls. I'm going to pursue far more cold-blooded creatures." Clearly he meant fish. He's a well known angler.'

Haseke had listened attentively as she had told about her meeting with the senator in Stockholm, about the attempts on his life, about the secrecy and security precautions surrounding him. He knew well who Senator Stockwell was. Everyone did; the senator was becoming world famous for his struggle for world peace. He also knew that Stockwell was a decent angler. A few months ago he had read the senator's book about trout fishing in Kashmir.

'Their assassination attempt has a far better chance of succeeding than a car bomb does,' he said. 'As far as I can see, it's the perfect assassination plot. When the flood comes, it won't make any difference how extensive the security precautions are around him. No one stands a chance of surviving.'

'What do we do?' asked Anna. 'We have to warn them.'

'How do we go about it?' said Ken. 'Should we catch a ptarmigan and train it to be a carrier pigeon?'

Haseke wondered how much of Ken's inappropriate humour stemmed from nervousness.

'Can't we walk there?' asked Anna.

'In this weather?' The major motioned towards the rain and darkness outside. 'The way there is too far and rough. It's not easy to follow the path even in broad daylight. Besides, they've taken our shoes. In this terrain you can't get far without something to protect your feet.'

Haseke nodded in agreement. He knew that the shoe problem could be solved provisionally. But without a map or any familiarity with the area, the venture was hopeless.

'But we must do something,' said Anna. 'We simply can't watch them blast the dam and kill us all. Not to speak of what a catastrophe it would be if they succeed in killing the senator. Millions of people have pinned their hopes on him.'

'You're already speaking of him in headlines,' said Ken. 'Mankind's only hope for survival. I know you write that sort of rubbish. But surely you don't believe it?'

'Maybe it will mean something for the cause of world peace if we save the senator,' said Haseke. 'Maybe not. It makes no difference which opinion we have; in either case we must do something. Our lives also are at stake: we also die with the blast. Steiner and Moll don't have the slightest intention of leaving behind any witnesses who can identify them afterwards. I'm sure they have a plan of escape all prepared.'

'In that case why haven't they shot us already?' said Ken. 'That must mean they don't plan to kill us.'

'Perhaps they want the whole thing to seem like an accident,' said Haseke. 'As if it were a natural bursting of the dam. A Swedish scandal. A catastrophe for the country's engineering reputation. In that case, they can't shoot us. They can only use pistols to keep us in check. At the decisive moment they'll probably lock us in somewhere and let the flood take care of the killing.'

'They said nothing would happen to us if we behaved,' said Anna.

'Jesus!' Peter Baxter suddenly got up from the major's bed. 'How naïve can you get? They said nothing would happen to us! They're lying. Why should they hesitate to lie? They haven't hesitated to kill.'

He breathed heavily and pressed his hands hard against his diaphragm. His eyes darted around the room as if he were looking for a way to escape. Haseke recognized the symptoms. This man was fear-stricken. The pressure was too much for him.

'Jesus!' he said again. 'Don't you understand what's happening? They're going to lock us in and drown us! Drown us like cats!'

'We must try to remain calm,' said Haseke.

Peter stroked his hair nervously. Then he took a deep breath as if he were about to dive. He forced a thin smile.

'Forgive me,' he said.

He turned his back on them and left the room.

In the silence that followed, they could hear his footsteps down the corridor and then a door farther down the corridor opened and closed. Peter Baxter was in his bedroom. Alone with his fear.

Haseke understood why he had left. The varnish had cracked and he did not want to expose publicly what was underneath.

Weakness was something one only revealed within the close family circle and hardly even there. Peter Baxter was weak; Haseke had known this long before he had been put to the test. Weak was perhaps not the right word. Rather, he was a man who had given up. Haseke wondered why those people who had most difficulty living also had most difficulty dying.

'They must be Communists.' The major broke the silence.

'Why?' asked Anna. 'It seems to me they don't believe in anything at all.'

'I mean, the people behind it all. They have a lot to gain by killing an American politician in Sweden. It could completely destroy Sweden's relationship with the USA. Just as a shot in Sarajevo destroyed the relationship between Austria and Serbia.'

'I don't think that's right,' said Anna. 'I think they're out to get him because of his peace propaganda.'

'That would also suggest Communists,' said the major. 'They've always preached peace far and wide, but have secretly been working for war. In Korea and Vietnam. In Africa. In South America. In Cuba. It would be just like them, I think, to negotiate peace with the senator while at the same time trying to kill him as soon as he has some success.'

'There could also be American interest lying behind the plan,' said Haseke. 'The American armament industry is very powerful. If it felt threatened by an over-enthusiastic disarmament movement, it would clamp down. Besides, political murders are an American tradition.'

'That's also how I interpreted the senator,' said Anna. 'When I asked him about who lay behind the attempts on his life, he answered "The armament industries in the East and West". But I felt he added the bit about the East simply for the sake of balance.'

'The capitalist system is rotten all the way through,' said Ken. 'Especially in the USA. They need wars to keep the industry booming. It was a tough day for Wall Street when the Korean War ended. A man like Senator Stockwell must be the capitalist society's number one enemy.'

'It makes no difference what we think,' said the major. 'We must do something. We can't just sit here talking. We must act. And we must act now.'

He raised his glass and drank from it. Haseke had noticed that the major's self-confidence had returned after the fifth glass of whisky. Now it was blossoming. Haseke hoped it would not wither away from excessive nourishment.

'Attack,' said the major. 'Attack is our best defence. We stand a good chance of defeating the enemy if we take advantage of the surprise factor. In addition, if we can neutralize their advantage of firearms, then it's nearly settled.'

'Have you thought of how to neutralize their firearms?' said Ken. 'Plug up the pistols?'

'The enemy rely on their weapons,' said the major. 'They know that with the pistols they can defeat any unarmed attack. They know we daren't attack them. We won't try either. We'll attack their room. We'll transform their safe hide-out into a prison from which they can't escape.'

'How?' Haseke was becoming interested.

'The room has a window and a door. The window has heavy shutters which could easily be shut and barricaded from outside. They could never get out that way.'

'But the door,' said Haseke. 'It's an ordinary interior door. Moll could kick through it in a few minutes.'

'Quite right. But a few minutes would be too late. The whole kitchen would be ablaze. That's the main point of my plan. We block the windows with the shutters. We block the door with flames. There's a can of petrol in the workshop. There's enough to make the kitchen go up in flames. They'll get their bang, these two fellows. But not the way they'd planned.'

'It's arson,' exclaimed Anna.

'It's either our lives or theirs. This is war, young lady. Crush the enemy or you'll be destroyed. Those are the conditions of war.'

'Old Clausewitz is out haunting again,' said Ken. 'It's incredible that this stone-dead war theorist has been kept alive among you officers. You still believe that stuff about crushing the enemy. You've learned nothing. Even the Vietnam war made no impression on you, when the world's most powerful nation couldn't crush one of the smallest, despite its enormous superiority. I'll bet you haven't even heard of Sun Tzu.'

'Who's that?'

'Sun Tzu. He lived in China nearly three thousand years ago. But he's still not dead. It was by applying his military strategy that the Vietnamese people succeeded in winning the war with the USA. Sun Tzu is the opposite of Clausewitz. Use as little violence as possible, he says. Fight your enemy with other means: divide the enemy, undermine his morale, attack his strategy.'

'Theories,' said the major. 'Just theories. Typical of young people today. All theories, no experience.'

'You're wrong again. I'm the one who's had experience, not you. I was in Vietnam for two years. As a soldier. Then I split. I'm a living example of Sun Tzu: undermine the enemy's morale. My morale became so undermined that I deserted.'

'I thought you were an ordinary Swedish photographer.'

'Sorry to disappoint you.'

'So, you're a deserter, you say. As if that would make you qualified to express yourself on military questions. I don't go along with that idea. I have no confidence in traitors.'

Ken stood up slowly.

'You military men are like scout masters,' he said. 'You're full of ideals that you want others to live up to.'

'I don't want to generalize,' said the major. 'But one can't ignore certain universal truths. For example, that deserters are untrustworthy.'

'Deserting is the only decent thing a man who's landed in a war can do.' said Ken. 'That applied to the Vietnam war in the highest degree. It also applies to your little war, Major. Don't count on my co-operation. Goodnight.'

He went out of the room.

'What damned treachery,' said the major.

'Because he didn't want to take part in arson?' Anna was upset. 'I don't know if I agree. If we'd taken a vote in a democratic fashion, then I'm convinced most of us would have acted like Ken. Voted no.'

'Democracy is all well and good,' said the major. 'But right now we don't have time for such childishness!'

'Democracy can never be childish,' said Anna.

'In a crisis what you need is a firm hand and not lots of talk. And your attitude to my plan of attack doesn't interest me. You're a woman. This has nothing to do with you.'

'In a crisis what you need is co-operation,' said Anna. 'Not a dictator.'

'You're disturbing us,' said the major. 'I suggest you go to bed. Goodnight!'

'I was just leaving. Goodnight.'

She stood up and left.

Haseke felt a strong desire to follow Anna's example. It was a bad sign that all the young people had left. But he stayed. There was something in the major's plan. It was simple and therefore practicable, and besides, it led straight to the point. If it succeeded, it would free them from all their problems at one blow. It didn't bother his conscience that the plan aimed at killing Steiner and Moll. Naturally he detested all violence. But if he were faced with the alternative of killing someone or being killed himself, the choice was very simple. And he knew that he was faced by this alternative.

'And you, Doctor Haseke,' said the major. 'Are you also planning to retreat?'

'I'm staying. I think your plan might succeed. What would my responsibility be?'

'The window shutters.'

'I accept.'

'Good,' said the major. 'We'll do it this way.'

Before he started to outline his plan in detail, he refilled his glass once again. He drank a big gulp. Haseke watched him and thought that everyone had his own way of killing the maggots which consumed him inside.

14

THE MAJOR STOOD in the corridor and looked towards the main building. He could see into the dining room and kitchen. Nothing had moved in there during the last half hour. The rain had let up and the heavy thunderclouds were dispersing. It grew lighter and lighter. It was the beginning of August and the northern lights were still just like twilight. The midnight sun only made quick dips below the horizon, although in a few months' time the sun would disappear completely, as if drowned.

The major felt confident. He could not be blamed for what had happened. It was not his fault that the fishing lodge had become the scene for a political assassination. He had now completely given up the idea of rescuing the tourist scheme. Out of the ruins of the former tourist representative emerged the unbroken military officer. Determined to save his own skin and that of the others. By means of a ruthless attack on the assassins.

He had the whisky glass with him. He drank carefully. He knew he could not stand an endless amount. Alcohol had been his companion for years. It relaxed him. It freed him from the feeling that hours crept by like snails while years raced by like express trains. It gave him a comfortable impression of being a mere spectator of his own actions. As if everything happened at a distance. As if the present were a memory at the same time as it was in progress.

Still nothing from the main building, not a sound, not a glimpse of movement. The major was convinced. The men in Grahn's room were asleep.

He left his post at the corridor window and went into his room. Haseke sat there waiting. The major nodded to him.

'Let's get started.'

Carefully he opened his window and climbed out. Haseke followed him. The major pointed at the window shutters.

'Look here,' he said. 'Take a look at the fastenings behind the shutters. They're each held open by a hasp.'

Haseke leaned towards the wall and looked up into the space between the shutter and the wall.

'Loosen the hasps, slam the shutters quickly, and as soon as they're shut, put up the iron crossbar!'

The major undid the hasp holding one shutter against the wall and pointed out a strong iron bar.

'This fastens into a hook on the other shutter. When it's fastened no one can open the shutters from the inside. The shutters on Grahn's window are the same. Does your watch have a second hand?'

Haseke showed him a strong wristwatch of steel with a red second hand clearly visible in the twilight.

'It's now twelve thirty. We'll set zero hour for 00.50 Ten to one.' The major set his watch forward one minute to tally with Haseke's.

'Exactly at 00.50, we'll attack. Twenty minutes from now. Unfasten the hasps, close the shutters, put up the iron bar! There's an iron ladder under the window. Lean it against the shutters as an added protection. Repeat!'

'Zero hour is 00.50. On the second I close the shutters and put up the iron crossbar. Then I take the ladder from under the window and lean it against the shutters.'

'Good. Make sure the ladder is steady so that it can't slip. It must be properly braced against the ground.'

Haseke nodded.

'I'm going to move now. You wait here until before zero hour. Good luck.'

He turned his back on Haseke, walked along the long wall of the guest cottage and turned at the corner. With slow steps he proceeded along the gabled side. The grass was wet. In no time at all his socks were soaking wet. He bent down and took them off. He peered around the corner at the window in the main building. He laughed to himself. The irony of fate. During most of his life he had trained to participate in war without ever having the opportunity to show what he was worth under real conditions. In all the mock wars he had carried out with the practice units or on paper, he had never been able to assert himself with the brilliance he had wished. His career had lagged behind. His promotion had been slow.

And now! When he had resigned and had adapted himself to a civilian career, this happened. He had landed right in the midst of the action. He would show those armchair soldiers what he was worth in the field! He laughed again.

Still nothing from the main building. The only noise he heard was the remote roar of the river, and every now and then a low rumble from the distant thunder.

With quiet, stealthy steps he moved across the yard. He concentrated on not being heard. It was impossible not to be seen. It was far too light. If someone was keeping watch behind the windows of the main cabin, the major would be discovered even if he crawled across the yard.

He reached the workshop door, slowly pressed down the handle, opened it and slipped inside. Under the white sheet over a camp bed was outlined the bulky shape of the dead housekeeper.

Was there a faint smell?

He was overpowered by the desire to be sick.

But just for an instant. There in a corner stood the petrol can, next to a power saw. He picked it up and felt it. It was full.

Quietly he crept out of the workshop, crouching as he passed the windows of the dining room on his way to the entrance. He went up the steps.

This was the critical moment.

Would the door be locked?

He tried the handle. The door opened. Slowly, very slowly, he went into the main building.

In the dark dining room chairs and tables stood as if they had been abandoned for ever. A feeling of quiet desolation brooded under the roof. He moved slowly towards the kitchen. Carefully he put one foot down, shifted his weight, put down the other foot.

A floorboard creaked.

He froze. Was it a coincidence? He had never heard this floor creak before. But he knew that completely different noises dominate the night and the day.

He stood still in the middle of the floor. Had Steiner and Moll woken? But there was no sound from their room. Carefully he began to creep forward again.

Again the floor creaked.

At the boundary between the dining room and the kitchen a floorboard groaned.

The major stiffened. At any instant the two men might come dashing through the door. With raised pistols. They wouldn't hesitate when they caught sight of him. He listened tensely. He was ready to flee at the slightest sound.

Nothing happened. It stayed quiet in Grahn's room. The major placed the petrol can on the floor.

He looked at his watch. 00.46. Four minutes left. He unscrewed the top of the can. He stuck his hand in his pocket. The matches were there.

Three minutes left.

He looked around. From the spot where he stood in the kitchen, he had a view of the yard. He would be able to see Haseke coming across the yard.

Two minutes left.

Behind the white door at the back of the kitchen Steiner and Moll slept without a clue about what awaited them. His conscience did not bother him about burning them in there. They were the ones who had started the war and now the law of war prevailed: kill or be killed. He was sure that the fire would start an explosion. There was more than enough petrol in the can to set both houses violently ablaze. Steiner and Moll did not stand a chance.

One minute left.

Haseke came creeping from the guest cottage. Silently he moved across the yard and disappeared from the major's sight.

Half a minute left.

The major took the nearest kitchen chair, picked it up off the floor and carried it cautiously to the door of Grahn's room. He held the chair up in the air and waited.

The window shutters slammed shut. He heard the bang clearly through the closed door. The iron crossbar was up.

He pushed the chair under the handle. Perfect fit. The door was blocked. He ran back, took the can, tipped it over. The contents poured out. He grabbed the curtains and tugged. The rod broke, the chequered material tumbled down on to the floor and absorbed the liquid.

Now the matches.

He pulled out the matchbox, struck a match alight and tossed it on to the flood on the floor.

It sizzled and died.

A knock from inside made the door bulge. Moll had awoken.

A new match.

It died too, when it landed in the liquid on the floor.

The door splintered with a crash. The chair flew across the floor and hit the opposite wall.

The third match.

The major lit it and set alight the whole box which flared up in his hand. He held it to the soaking curtain material. It charred, but did not catch fire.

Moll rushed through the broken door like a streak of lightning. Before the major could get up from his stooping position on the floor, Moll was upon him. He hit the major with the backside of his hand. A backhander against the carotid artery just behind his right ear.

15

THERE IS NOTHING worse than waking up from a nightmare and, before heaving even one sigh of relief, being hit with an even greater horror: reality. In his sleep, Haseke had tried to run away from an oncoming flood which pursued him and destroyed everything in its path. When it caught up with him and engulfed him, he woke up. At first he felt an instant of release, and then he remembered the night's terrible events. He saw before him the major's limp body which Moll, with the help of the panic-stricken Peter Baxter, had carried out of the main building and heaved into the workshop as if it had been a sack of refuse. And even worse. He could still hear Sabine's scream, when Moll had dragged her out of bed.

After the major's unsuccessful attack, Haseke had stood in the yard with Steiner's pistol in his back. He had been unable to intervene when Moll came carrying Sabine. She reached her arms out to him and begged him to help her, and then screamed and screamed until she was suddenly silent somewhere inside the main building. The silence tortured him as much as her screams.

'You've disobeyed my orders,' said Steiner. 'We'll take Fräulein Krämer as a hostage. I hope you understand what will happen, if you or anyone else does something thoughtless again.'

'Pig,' was all Haseke had replied.

He touched his neck where Steiner had hit him with the pistol barrel as an answer. It felt sore. But it was no longer bleeding.

He also remembered Anna's and Ken's frightened faces, when he had entered the guest cottage after Steiner had released him. Peter, whom Moll had summoned to help him carry the major's corpse, had explained to them what had happened: that the major had been killed; that Sabine had been taken hostage. Haseke had gone into his room. His greatest asset in life was that he could sleep when he needed. He could not solve anything. He had taken part in a battle and lost. He had been forced to submit to the victor's conditions. At least for the present. He had fallen asleep within a quarter of an hour.

He opened the curtains and looked out on a brilliantly sunny day. A lovely day to die. A great deal suggested that this would be his last day. Before nightfall his nightmare about the flood would come true. Steiner and Moll would blow up the dam and drown them all.

Unless he could prevent them.

He felt surprised and giddy about the course of events. About how the idyll had changed into a bloody drama. Yet he was not astonished. He had always had the feeling that violence would catch up with him in the end. That death would become his daily companion yet again.

He remembered the last spring of the war in Berlin. How he had taken part in the defence as a lieutenant in a company of boy soldiers, not much more than a boy himself. How after the collapse he had prowled through the ruins in an even tougher struggle for survival. He remembered how he had focused his life just on one goal; keeping himself alive long enough to see the crocuses bloom.

He had been nineteen at the time, but his feeling for crocuses had stayed with him through the years. Every spring he set himself the same goal. Peace and prosperity in Germany today seemed to him an abnormal state, pleasant but accidental. For someone who had grown up in a city while it was slowly being destroyed, violence and death would always be part of life's normal conditions. Perhaps the death which he had so miraculously avoided that time had now caught up with him. It did not terrify him. Quite the opposite. It was near death that he felt truly alive.

He devoted himself to shaving with the same ritual precision as an ancient samurai preparing himself for battle. He looked at himself in the mirror, saw the wrinkles on his brow, the furrows around his mouth, the grey temples, the grey beard. To age was to become an inferior copy of what one had once been. But the strength was still left. And the will to survive.

He dressed in clean underpants, a clean shirt, clean socks and pulled on a pair of light uniform trousers which were left over from the war. Then he found an extra pair of inner soles for his boots, stuffed each of them into a thick skiing sock and pulled them on. The trick of double socks with a felt sole in between was also a memory from the war, a memory of quiet advances in the dark. It was no longer a problem that he had been deprived of his shoes.

On the bench outside the workshop sat Moll, in a chequered shirt, with his back against the wall. When he caught sight of Haseke, he put his hand on his pistol which he had shoved down into his belt. Ken stood with his hands in his pockets and looked down at the river. Through the open window of the kitchen a triad sounded like a doorbell in a modern house. Haseke understood from the crackling noise that the triad was a radio signal, the daily communication test with Kiruna. A businesslike woman's voice called:

'Paktas Lodge from three six, Paktas Lodge from three six!'

'Paktas Lodge here.' It was Anna speaking.

'Testing. How are you out there? Good weather? Any luck fishing?'

'All's well.'

'Sounds good. Have a good time. Over and out.'

The triad sounded again. Ken looked at Haseke and shrugged his shoulders. There was nothing to be done. Anna came out of the main building with the same gesture.

'What could I do?' she said.

'How's Sabine?' asked Haseke.

'She sat looking out through the window the whole time I was there,' said Anna. 'I didn't have a chance to talk to her.'

'Did it look as if she'd been badly treated?'

'I don't think so. Steiner has the usual attitude towards women.

It shows in his manner. I mean, despite the pistol and the fact that he's planning to drown us, it's obvious he likes women.'

'That's what I feared.'

'No, not that way.'

'It's different with Moll,' said Ken, in a low voice so that Moll could not hear him. ' I think that fellow has rape in his eyes when he looks at you. Have you noticed how he stares at you?'

'Yes,' said Anna. 'I shudder just to think of it. Pig's bristles on his hands.'

'I'd like to talk to you about something privately,' Haseke said to Anna.

'Whoops,' said Ken. 'I'd better go down to the river then. I wonder how Peter's fishing is. His hands are probably trembling so much that the trout are missing the hooks.'

He started walking down to the river. Peter Baxter stood about one hundred metres upstream from the Table Rock. He was in the process of casting.

Haseke led Anna a little way down the slope. He indicated a rock and they sat down next to each other.

'Everything's like a nightmare,' said Anna. 'Do you think we have a chance of surviving?'

'Maybe.'

He looked at her. She seemed quite calm and collected. Her eyes were steady even if the pupils were somewhat dilated. Her hands did not tremble at all even if they moved a bit uneasily in her lap. Panic had not yet struck her and begun its breakdown.

'I need your help,' he said. 'I'm planning to make an attempt to take Moll unawares. As you can see, he's much stronger than I am. It means that I must get him in a position where he can't take advantage of his bodily strength. You can help me do this.'

'Why not Ken?' she asked. 'He's twice as strong as I am. And not half as scared.'

'I need a woman.'

'Oh, it depends on sex. The strong sex tamed by the fair one. Samson and Delilah. In an unguarded moment out with the scissors and clip, clip! It won't work that way. Even you don't believe it.'

'That's the basic idea, I admit. But it's not so much Delilah I'm asking you to play, as another woman from the Bible:

Susanna in the bath. I've cast Moll in the role of the excited and curious man. The only discomfort you'll have to undergo is getting a little wet. And Moll's ogling, of course. I'll take care of the rest.'

16

HE'D KNOWN THE whole time that she would say yes. But he had never guessed that she would reveal herself to be so beautiful when she undressed. Beautiful in the classical sense, with full breasts, wide hips, slender limbs and the suppleness of a female native. Perhaps he would have to change his opinion of her. He had taken her for one of those nordic career women who consider a marriage proposal as an implication that they cannot look after themselves and a pregnancy as spiritual death at a young age. There was a primitive quality in Anna, a basic womanliness, which would surely prevail over the career woman when the time came.

Anna had undressed on the farthest tip of the Table Rock, which jutted out a few metres into the river, low and wide like a landing-stage. Beyond it the water rushed past, violent and foaming, on its way to the Grand Rapids about thirty metres farther downstream. On the leeward side of the Table Rock, the water lay calm and still in a natural cove. Anna sat down on the rock and began to splash her feet in the water. Then she leaned back on her elbows, closed her eyes, thrust her breasts forwards and sprawled out invitingly to the sun like a model for a nudist brochure. Or so it would seem to Moll's dirty mind, hoped Haseke.

He himself reclined in the grass about twenty metres above her. He was sorry that he could not admire her loveliness undisturbed, but he had to consider her as delicious bait for an ugly fish like Moll. He wondered if Moll had noticed Anna. If he was already on his way down. But he did not turn his head to take a look.

He looked out over the river. He considered all streams as

individuals, all different from each other, always changing. He had many friends among them, no enemies, but for many he had great respect. Not as an angler, of course. An angler's acquaintance with a body of water in which he fished was only an acquaintance with the surface. Rather as a canoe paddler. Haseke also went in for white-water canoeing, a sport which forced its practiser into direct contact with the water. Often a contact with its depths. Each summer he spent a week in the Möll and the Lieser, two of the rivers with sources in the melting snows around the Grossglockner.

How long would it take Moll to come down here? Would he come at all? Would the plan go without a hitch? All he could do was wait.

He remembered how he had capsized in the Lieser when he was there at the end of May, how he had been swept along in the whirling body of water until he had crawled ashore many hundred metres downstream, soaked right through by the water. But also by happiness. Untamed water was his element.

He noticed that Anna cast a quick look up at the house. He tried to read her face. Was Moll coming? Probably not. Anna seemed completely unaffected. She relaxed again in her nakedness, alone with the sun.

He wondered how difficult the Grand Rapids could be. They began about thirty metres downstream from the Table Rock and went on for about one hundred metres. They were like a summary of the three most difficult sections in the Möll, which he knew inside out. First, a stretch with waves of currents making walls like the Moser waves. Afterwards, a drop of two hundred metres between a pair of cliffs down into a boiling cauldron like the Kolbnitz Hole. And last, two powerful streams which came from each side and met in a tremendous whirlpool like the Mühldorf Gulf. He felt quite at home with the Grand Rapids.

Suddenly Anna began to move. She slipped into the water of the calm cove below the Table Rock.

That was the sign.

Moll had bit.

Steps were heard in the grass. Moll was already approaching. Anna had seen him late.

Anna lowered herself in the water with her back against the

shore. She splashed water on her legs with her hand. The reflections from the water played on her skin. Her body was evenly tanned all over.

Moll went past him without a glance and stopped on the shore. Anna lowered herself in the water up to her hips. Haseke admired her. The water temperature could not be more than ten degrees centigrade. She splashed water over her body. Then she rose in a rain of glittering drops of water and turned around.

'Oh,' she screamed, as if she'd just discovered her observer. She threw one arm in front of her breasts and the other hand over the womb in the classic pose of an embarrassed woman.

'Aren't you ashamed?' she shouted at Moll. She had to shout to make herself heard above the din of the rapids.

'Take it easy, baby,' Moll shouted back. He laughed. 'I'm not dangerous.'

'There,' shouted Anna and pointed to the Table Rock. 'Give me my towel.'

She'd put her large towel on the farthest tip of the Table Rock. Moll looked at it. Then he looked up towards Haseke sitting on the grass slope twenty yards away. He put his hand on the pistol butt in his belt.

'Give me my towel!' Anna shouted from the water, still covering her breasts and womb with her arms and hands.

Moll laughed again.

'Can't you see I'm freezing?'

'OK, baby,' shouted Moll. 'Your towel's coming up.'

He went out on to the Table Rock. He turned around and glared at Haseke. Then he bent over to pick up the towel.

That instant Haseke took off, dashing down the grass slope. Hand on pistol butt. Pistol up out of the belt. Too late.

Haseke hurled himself forward in a flying tackle at Moll's waist. His shoulder crashed into Moll's stomach. In a wide arc both men fell into the river.

The impact was like a slap from a giant hand. They sank below the surface. At first Haseke lost hold of Moll, but then he grabbed his legs, around the hollows of his knees. Ice-cold water everywhere, in mouth, nose, ears.... They tussled together, Moll kicking and kicking. The current dragged them with it.

They were swirled down to the Grand Rapids. Haseke arched

his back in order to pull Moll under him, and pressed down with all his might. Then he needed air. He let go, stuck his head up above the surface and took a breath. Then he grabbed Moll again. They came into the high waves, both of them tossing up and down as they were swept onwards.

Towards the falls and down into the Cauldron. Haseke struggled to keep Moll underneath. Moll was still kicking, jerking his body and flailing his arms in an attempt to surface and get air. Haseke held him down.

Haseke's shoulder hit stone and he lost his grip. Moll came up and screamed at the sky. Haseke grabbed his throat, pressing with all his strength and twisting him underneath. They whirled onwards.

Their speed increased and the current forced them downwards. Haseke hit his neck on a stone. He was losing strength, but did not loosen his grasp. They scraped against the bottom. The freezing cold pierced them to the marrow. There was no more air; their lungs were about to burst. The torrent tossed them onwards.

Moll's kicking ceased, and he lay lifeless in Haseke's arms. Haseke swam a stroke with one arm and came up to the surface. Air. Blue sky. Moll floated motionlessly by his side. Haseke began to kick with his legs to reach the shore.

Then it happened.

With a tug, Moll twisted around in the water and broke loose. Haseke continued alone. He turned over in the water and floated on his back, feet first, the regulation position for fast water. He was completely exhausted. He had lost. He gave up.

He opened his eyes and discovered willow trees by his side. Stones scraped against his back. He had been washed ashore. He grasped a stone and pulled himself towards land. He turned over on to his stomach and crawled on his hands and knees up on to the shore.

The water ran out of his nose and mouth. His stomach turned inside out. He retched over the stones on the beach.

With great effort he raised his head.

Where was Moll?

He heard a footstep. Someone came wading through the water behind him. He gathered his strength and started to get up on all fours.

17

She tripped and fell headlong and the stones rushed towards her hitting her elbows and knees. She scrambled up again and continued her staggering run over the stones on the shore of the river. She was barefoot and she stubbed her toes, scraped the soles of her feet. She was naked. In her hand she held the towel which she had grabbed before rushing after the two men.

She was tired. Her feet ached. She tried in vain to keep pace with the current, but the men in the water were swept away with a speed with which she could not keep up. Soon they had disappeared from view. She ran onwards on unsteady ankles, her heavy breathing drowning out the river's roar.

The willows grew closer and closer to the water's edge, until she was forced to stop running. The willows whipped her thighs, stomach and breasts.

Then she saw him. Haseke lay on the beach, face downward and arms outstretched, as if he had fallen from a great height. Still alive. He lifted his head with difficulty. Let it drop again.

Where was Moll?

She wanted to shout, but it was pointless. The noise level of the river was too high. She continued onward. She was forced to wade out into the water to avoid a group of willows that grew all the way down to the water.

Suddenly the man in front of her heaved himself up on all fours as if he had heard her coming. With his back towards her, he got up and, staggered sideways like a drunkard making a last effort to stay on his feet; then he turned to face her. His eyes were closed, his face was twisted, and he held his hand raised behind his shoulder.

Anna stopped. There were just a few metres between them. In the raised hand, he held a huge stone ready to be thrown.

He opened his eyes to aim, stopped halfway through the throw, blinked his eyes, gaped and dropped the stone. With a crash, it hit the stones on the shore.

'You,' he said. 'Is it you?'

She saw him staring at her body, remembered that she was naked and wrapped the towel about her.

'Have you seen Moll?' asked Haseke.

She shook her head.

'He got away!'

Haseke stood more steadily now. He seemed to recover quickly. Through his soaking clothing one could see the outline of his body strong and in good condition like a young man's. His breath came more easily.

'He got away!' Haseke shouted, and made a wild gesture towards the river. 'Moll got away!'

He looked around, scanning the shore on which they stood, then shifting his eyes to the opposite shore. He looked at the willows behind them and she was struck by an acute fear that Moll might suddenly come rushing out of this thick greenery.

'Where's he gone?' shouted Haseke.

Suddenly Anna noticed that she was cold, and started back along the shore in the direction of her clothes. She felt drained. The tremendous tension she had been under had not let up. It had simply changed into emptiness. Into uncertainty about what had happened. She had played the main part in a drama which had to come to an end.

Carefully she placed her feet on one stone after another. The soles of her feet felt sore at every step. Once again, the willows forced her out into the water.

From the corner of her eye she glimpsed something green-checked in the whirlpools.

She stopped.

Checks did not occur in nature. She waded out into the water far enough to be sure.

The green checks were Moll's shirt.

Moll was inside it. Drowned.

He was hanging in midstream on a broken willow branch, which was stuck between two rocks. The branch had wedged itself under his belt and pinned him against the rocks like a speared seal. He lay face downwards, his clothes and hair fluttering in the rapids as if in a hard wind.

Suddenly Haseke stood next to her in the water and she leaned on him with infinite relief. He put his arm around her shoulders and, without thinking, she surrendered to a childlike need for security and let herself sink upon his chest. His hand stroked her hair, she put her arms around his waist and squeezed up against him. When his mouth pressed against the skin of her throat and his hand slid upwards and stopped on one of her breasts, she felt all her childlike needs become very womanly and turned her face up towards his.

Just then she slipped, staggered and drew Haseke with her in a tottering dance over the stones on the bottom. Suddenly she felt how ice-cold the water was around her legs and feet. Haseke took her hand and led her ashore. A cloud of mosquitoes attacked immediately. She looked at her skin. It was covered with pink blotches. She had been attacked by mosquitoes for a long time without noticing it.

'Did you see where the pistol landed?' he asked.

'Jesus, so many mosquitoes,' she said.

'The pistol. I must have the pistol. Or I can't tackle Steiner.'

'It landed in the water. It hit a stone. Then it slipped into the water right next to where I was standing.'

He turned his back on her and began to run along the shore, towards the Table Rock. She noticed that he had thick socks on his feet. She staggered after him. Despair rose within her. Once again she was left behind. Once again she was the victim of men's actions. She made a great effort to suppress the panic growing within her. She slowed her pace, slowly and methodically placing her feet on the stones which seemed steadiest.

A shot echoed against the mountainside on the other side of the river, and Anna started to run. It could not be Haseke who was shooting. Although he had disappeared from sight ahead of her, he could not have reached the Table Rock yet. Much less could he have managed to fish up the pistol.

The willows thinned out and she got a clear view of the river, the shore and the slope up to the cottages.

Steiner came running down the path with the pistol in his hand.

She stopped.

Haseke was not visible. Had he been shot?

Then she saw his head emerge from the water right next to the Table Rock. He had reached it. He looked up at the running Steiner.

Steiner stopped, raised his pistol and fired.

Haseke disappeared underwater. But she did not think the shot had hit. The distance was more than one hundred metres.

Steiner continued down the path.

Haseke surfaced again next to the Table Rock. Steiner stopped again and shot. The bullet exploded against a stone only a metre away from Haseke's head. Haseke ducked underwater. Steiner ran on. The next time Haseke surfaced, he would be near enough to hit.

The water splashed violently, Haseke stood up, dashed towards land and threw himself down on the shore with a black object in his hand. He had found the pistol.

A loud bang. Steiner stopped upright, turned left and squatted behind a rock. He aimed and fired.

Haseke got on his feet and ran in the direction of Anna, while Steiner fired shot after shot at him. He threw himself down in a hollow in the ground and returned fire. One shot, not more. Then he got up again and dashed up the slope while Steiner fired. Once again he ducked down and took a shot.

Anna understood what Haseke was up to. Sabine. He was making a flanking movement around Steiner to reach the cottage before him and release her.

Steiner left the rock and began to run back up the path. Now it was Haseke's turn to shoot. Steiner did not take cover, but continued upwards. He was not stupid. Like Anna, he had spotted Haseke's intention.

The fight was over. The distance between the two men was so great that all shooting was pointless. The river's roar penetrated Anna's eardrums once again, her feet began to ache, and the mosquitoes were attacking relentlessly.

Steiner disappeared between the buildings in the yard. Haseke came up to Anna.

'I must release her,' he said. 'Sooner or later.'

He looked at the pistol. Turned it over in his hand.

'The pistol is the worst weapon I know. Completely useless, except at very close range. Preferably one should be close enough to press the muzzle against the enemy's forehead.'

Standing in front of her with straggling hair and dirty clothes, he filled Anna with admiration. After everything he had been through, he was still the same. He had the same calm facial expression as when he had been standing in the river fishing, completely undisturbed; he spoke with the same tone as when he had been conversing about the weather during breakfast; he observed her with the same steady gaze with which he had always looked at her. And, only a few minutes before, he had been fighting for his life. She admired him with all her heart. She felt a strong desire to reach out towards him.

But she controlled herself and was satisfied to observe the new side of herself which emerged now that civilization's thin covering had been stripped away: the instinct to turn to the strongest person, to seek a protector. First Ken and now Haseke. Probably a biological reaction. It would have to be in that case. The theoretical question of a woman's role did not interest her just then. Instead she said:

'What do we do now?'

He stuffed the pistol into his trouser waistband.

'What happens now is that you must protect yourself from the immediate danger.'

'Which one!'

'That the mosquitoes will eat you alive.'

18

'WHAT A STORY!' said Ken. 'If you'd only had a camera! Imagine the pictures you could have taken! Two men fighting for their lives in the rapids. A shoot-out at the foot of the mountain. Incredible!'

Anna dug her nails into the palm of her hand. She nearly burst into hysterical laughter over Ken's comments about the drama in which she had taken part. He saw everything from an exclusively professional point of view: good story, good pictures. To him what had happened was material for an article and not reality.

It occurred to her that the way she saw Ken now was perhaps how all subjects of her interviews had seen her as a journalist.

Ken and Peter had reached the Table Rock by the time Anna had put on her clothes. They had been a few hundred metres upstream when the first shot occurred, then they had watched the drama from a safe distance. Anna told them what had happened. How she had lured Moll out on to the Table Rock, how Haseke had heaved him into the river, how they had found Moll's drowned body, and how Haseke had recovered Moll's pistol in her bathing pool.

Ken was certainly right. It was an incredible story.

And now they stood by the side of the river while the mosquito armada attacked them from all sides. As usual, Peter said not a word. It was as if he lived in a house of passivity with shutters and doors closed against what happened around him. Haseke was also silent, but in a completely different way, as if he were gathering strength for new deeds. Ken did not seem to take it at all seriously. Probably this was his way of coping with reality.

'Here,' said Ken, and offered Anna a canister of mosquito repellent.

She took it and sprayed herself thoroughly. It was as if a glass wall were erected between the mosquitoes and herself.

She also felt as if there were a glass wall between herself and Ken. She had had that feeling all morning. Ken had treated her as if she were just anyone and not a woman with whom he had been intimate the night before. She had tried to reach him. He had not rejected her, but he had avoided her. He had given her a joke instead of the assurance she wanted in return for giving him hers.

'And now,' said Ken. 'What do we do now?'

'Steiner,' said Haseke, while spraying himself.

'Yes?'

'As long as Steiner remains in the cottage guarding Sabine, she's effective as a hostage. But he's here to carry out a mission, namely to blow up the dam. And he can't do that at the same time as he's guarding Sabine. Naturally, he can't take her with him up to the dam. Sooner or later, he must expose himself. That will be my opportunity. I'm going to get up there now and lie in wait in some suitable place. I have three shots left in my pistol. That'll do.'

'Steiner won't give in easily,' said Ken. 'And you can be sure of one thing. If you really do succeed in preventing him, his first move will be to kill Sabine.'

'I'm aware of the difficulties. But there's a chance that I can get at him when he has to do two things at once: guard Sabine and blow up the dam.'

'You Germans are incredible. You compose beautiful music like Beethoven and Mozart; you are dreamers and poets like Goethe and Hesse; but most of all, you are masters at letting all these good qualities go to hell and devoting yourselves to violence instead.'

'You're completely correct,' said Haseke. 'Even if our good qualities are superior to those of other countries, our bad qualities are worse. But we can't waste time on generalizations now. We must do something about a concrete situation. And that situation requires violence. I think I stand a good chance.'

'You are so head-over-heels indoctrinated with the capitalist heroic ideal that you can't see straight,' said Ken. 'Western civilization is threatened, you alone can rescue it. Saint George fighting the dragon, James Bond against Doctor Blofield, Doctor Haseke against gangster Steiner. Noble violence conquers evil violence. There's the reason for your endless wars, for your oppression of all dissidents, for your exploitation of undeveloped countries, your extortion of the working class. Good violence conquers evil violence. But there aren't two kinds of violence. There's only one. Evil violence.'

'What do you suggest?' said Haseke. 'We do something, or what?'

'Yes. I'm suggesting a simpler solution. Let's try Sun Tzu.'

They grew silent. Anna wondered, for an instant, if Ken were making another joke, but she set aside the thought. Sun Tzu was about the only thing Ken did not joke about.

Ken continued. 'Avoid all direct attacks, says Sun Tzu. They always weaken the attacker more than the attacked. Instead, find the enemy's weak point and take advantage of it. Get him off balance. When that's achieved, deliver the deathblow. That's the only violence necessary, says Sun Tzu. The last *coup de grâce*, the final deathblow.'

'What's the enemy's weak point?'

'The deadlocked position he's in. His aims are not the same as his possibilities. His aim is to explode the dam, but he has no possibility of doing this as long as you have a pistol to prevent him. His possibility is to kill Sabine, but that isn't his aim. There's nothing he'd rather do than trade. We'll meet him halfway. We'll offer him the dam in exchange for Sabine.'

'He'll never agree to that. Sabine is his only assurance against an attack from me.'

'He can get a new one.'

'Which?'

'A word of honour. You promise not to use the pistol against him or to prevent him from blasting the dam in any other way. In return, he hands over Sabine.'

'Word of honour! To a man like Steiner, a word of honour is just another trick!'

'True. But we offer our word of honour complete with a guarantee of its authenticity: my person.'

'I don't understand.'

'I suggest to Steiner the following deal: he releases Sabine in return for your promise to go up into the mountains with her and not return until everything's over. I guarantee the reliability of your word of honour with my presence. Of course he believes me. After all, I'm staking my life on it. Also it suits him to believe me. Now he can breathe freely. You and your pistol are out of the way. Now he can complete his mission.'

Anna wondered where Ken's sudden inclination for cold-blooded calculations had come from. Earlier he had done everything possible to keep out of things. Now he was diving right into the midst.

'Yes,' said Haseke. 'But we must prevent him from completing his mission.'

'That's exactly the purpose of my plan,' said Ken. 'The instant that Steiner exchanges Sabine for me, he exposes his weak point, which is that I'm not a harmless hostage like Sabine. I'm something quite different: an enemy who's managed to get close to him. He won't have any idea, but as a matter of fact he will already have lost the struggle by that time. The only thing remaining is the deathblow.'

Anna felt even more surprised. Ken was not only plunging right into the action, but suddenly he was taking over the leading role. Why this heroism? She saw him fish up a cigarette and light it with his lighter. Then he held the lighter up in front of the others.

'Look here! This is what happens when I offer Steiner a cigarette and offer him the lighter.'

He pressed the mechanism.

A light blue welding flame shot up thirty centimetres into the air.

'It's really a miniature flame-thrower,' he said. 'Before Steiner has time to recover from the shock, I've overpowered him.'

'But Steiner only smokes cigars,' Peter said suddenly.

'It makes no difference what he's lighting with this lighter.'

'But . . .?'

'No but. Don't you stick your nose in this! Hide behind Anna and shut up. Haseke and I will take care of this.'

Anna detested Ken's superior tone. His contempt for Peter applied to her as well. His disdain for everything womanly. She had not been told to shut up but it was understood: the woman was to remain silent in the meeting. These men made the rules with their own physical strength as the starting point: someone who could not perform men's actions could not participate in men's counsels either.

'Where did you get hold of such a handy contraption?' asked Haseke.

'At any tobacconist. This is an ordinary Ronson. All you have to know is how to deal with the nozzle of the gas container.'

'But if Steiner sees through the trick, what happens then?'

'Then we lose our stake in the game. But you needn't worry. The stake is me!'

Anna could not help smiling. These men! These boys! Right in the midst of their solid manliness they could still step back and make a little fun of themselves.

'And,' continued Ken, 'this is the beauty of it. If I die, you're still in a good position. Your Sabine is safe. You still have the pistol. Moreover you can feel inspired because a world-famous photographer has sacrificed himself on the altar of world peace.'

'Don't forget my word of honour.'

'You gave *me* your word of honour. You needn't keep your word with someone who's dead.'

'That's not correct. I gave my word of honour to Steiner. Through you.'

'OK, it makes no difference. I'll take care of Steiner.'

'You're taking enormous risks, Ken,' Anna couldn't help herself saying.

'A thug like Steiner is easy game for a disciple of Sun Tzu.' Ken laughed. Then he looked at Haseke. 'Shall we get started?'

'The plan is admirable,' said Haseke. 'If you can execute it as brilliantly as you planned it, Steiner doesn't stand a chance.'

Ken pointed at the mountain behind the buildings.

'Do you see that ravine up there? Nearly at the top?'

'Yes.'

'If I set Sabine free, climb up there with her. Then don't do anything to alarm Steiner. Stay there and wait. How long shall we say?'

He looked at his watch.

'It's eleven o'clock. Give me four hours. If I haven't returned by three o'clock, you can consider me . . .'

He turned his thumb down towards the ground.

'And,' he continued, 'if I finish him off earlier, I'll stand in the middle of the yard and wave. You can come down then.'

'I understand.'

Ken and Haseke began to climb the path, and Anna and Peter followed. Peter dawdled behind as if his passivity weighed down his feet. Suddenly Anna felt a violent anger rise within her and snapped at him to hurry up. The wounded look he gave her made her feel even more enraged.

'Steiner!'

Ken's shout resounded up the slope.

Haseke stopped on the path. Anna and Peter stopped behind him and Ken continued up to the building alone.

'Steiner!'

The window opened. Steiner and his pistol appeared in the window crack. Ken stood still.

'I'm coming up. I'm unarmed. I have a proposal to make to you.'

He continued upwards. Anna felt her anxiety growing. Her heart throbbed with alarm. Would Steiner shoot?

When Ken reached the lawn in front of the main building, he raised his hands over his head and stood still. He made a full turn, obviously at Steiner's orders.

Anna saw how both men began talking; Ken with his hands above his head, Steiner still half hidden inside the window. The whole time he pointed the pistol muzzle at Ken. Not a word of what was being said could be heard by the group waiting on the path.

Then Ken lowered his hands, went around the corner into the yard and disappeared inside the main building.

'Has he succeeded?' asked Anna.

'I think so,' said Haseke.

Then they stood silently on the path looking up at the house and waiting for what would happen. Time flowed as slowly as syrup. Anna saw how Haseke was clutching the pistol butt. Apparently his calm was due to self-control and not to his nature. Peter's hands fidgeted nervously in and out of his pockets. He could not stand still. Anna struggled against an impulse to snap at him again.

Sabine emerged between the buildings.

She ran across the yard, stumbling forward with her long hair in front of her face, straggly like hay. With one hand she wiped the tears from her eyes and in the other she held Haseke's shoes. She landed in his arms with a noisy sob, wailing about her misery. Luckily it was in German, thought Anna; so that she at least avoided the verbal accompaniment of this demonstration of the ultimate female weapon.

Haseke took Sabine by the shoulders and spoke firmly to her. Then he took his shoes from her, removed his outer pair of socks and put on his shoes, the whole time with a watchful eye on the cottages. He took Sabine by the hand and pulled her with him in the direction of the mountain.

When they had gone about fifty metres, Haseke stopped suddenly, turned around, and called to Peter.

Anna stood left alone while Peter dutifully hurried after. Why did Haseke call him and not her? Did she not count? Was she not even worth as much as Peter? Was she only useful as delicious bait in a trap, as a lamb to lure the lion?

Haseke spoke with Peter. Then he continued with Sabine up the slope. Peter came back.

'He's been thinking about what I said about Steiner's cigar,' he said.

'What else did he say?'

'He said that we shouldn't count on him any more. His first duty is to Sabine. He's going to stay out of danger with her. He advised us to do the same. But carefully, so that Steiner doesn't get suspicious.'

Anna felt completely abandoned. Haseke had left her to her fate. What would happen now if Steiner outwitted Ken? Peter would not be any help, rather the opposite.

Up on the mountain Haseke stopped suddenly. He turned around and waved his hand. Then he continued upwards with Sabine and did not turn around any more. Although Anna's eyes followed him the whole way.

19

'PUT THE ROD down here,' said Anna, pointing at the stones on the shore. Peter did as she said, as if he were a panic-stricken child. He had followed her down to the shore in the same way. They had stood there fishing for a while and then slowly moved with the current towards the willow grove. All this so that Steiner should not become suspicious if he glanced out of the window. Ken would have a hard enough time anyway when he tried to overpower Steiner.

They had now gone so far downstream that the willows hid them from the cottages.

'We'll crawl in here,' said Anna. 'Follow me.'

The willow grove was large enough to conceal a regiment. It extended over four hundred metres along the river and formed a half-circle up the slope, with its greatest breadth nearly two hundred metres. Anna was sure that Steiner would never be able to find her and Peter in there.

But the undergrowth was even more difficult to penetrate than she had thought. Under the thick foliage there was a tangle of stiff and bent branches which hardly left room enough for even the slenderest human body. Anna was heading for the edge of the woods which faced nearest the cottages. The distance through the willows was no more than thirty metres, but it took them half an hour to cover. They crept, wriggled, slithered, crawled, heaved and toiled forwards. When they reached the slope, they were completely torn by dried twigs; their faces were streaked from being whipped by lashing branches. But they were safe. If Steiner came after them, all they had to do was creep back a little way into the thick jungle. Here in the willows no one could find them.

Except the mosquitoes. They came in thick clouds through the willow branches, all equally bloodthirsty. Anna lent Peter the mosquito repellent time after time. It helped, but only for a short while. She wondered what all these mosquitoes lived off when she was not there.

Through the opening in the foliage she had a clear view up to the cottages. But so far the scene was empty and quiet. Both buildings stood there apparently empty of life. Behind them rose the mountains, lifeless backdrops. The sun glowered in its blue sky like an evil eye.

Anna was worried about Ken. She had been astonished by his clever plan to release Sabine and attack Steiner. She had been even more surprised that he himself was prepared to enter into the struggle.

She was ashamed to remember how she had interpreted his dismissive attitude during the morning when he refused to acknowledge their encounter of the night before. He had obviously been preoccupied with plans to deliver her and the others out of Steiner's and Moll's power. He had been in a man's world, a world where feelings are a threat against energy and risk-taking.

She was ashamed when she thought how she had suspected that

his non-violent ideology was simply a way of avoiding participation, much the same as his refusal to fight in the Vietnam war. At this very moment he was risking his life for her sake and that of the others.

She was filled with tenderness for him and recalled for an instant the strength of his embraces and the warmth of his skin. Then she was seized by an unreasonable anxiety. What kind of chance did Ken stand against a professional killer? None?

Next to her lay Peter. He was still as if numbed. He did what she told him, but took no initiative, said nothing, barely answered when she spoke to him.

'What's wrong with you?' she asked him irritably.

'What do you mean?' he answered quietly. He didn't meet her eyes.

'What's the matter with you?'

'Say it,' he said.

'Are you so afraid?'

'This makes me sick.'

He closed his eyes.

Anna looked at her watch. One and a half hours had passed since Ken had disappeared into the house. Should he not have already made an attempt at Steiner? Had it proved impossible? Or had he failed and been rendered helpless, maybe tied up? Was he sitting in there waiting to be put to death?

She sprayed with the aerosol can. The mosquitoes came closer and closer. If she had not had the spray, she would have been drained of blood long ago.

A flock of birds came flying over their hiding place and settled on the slope in front of them. They waddled about with sluggish bodies and quick head movements like haggling marketwomen. They must be ptarmigan.

A shot shattered the silence.

The ptarmigan flapped up into the air with wings beating hysterically and flew into the willow grove. Anna suddenly felt sick. Steiner was the only one of the two men in the house who had a pistol. Ken! Oh, Ken!

Panic struck her. Her life was at stake. In a little while Steiner would set out hunting. She would be the prey. Her heart began beating desperately. Death threatened her. Until now in her make-believe world death had not been real. It had been like the emergency exit in an auditorium. Something you knew was there, but that you did not count on having to face in the foreseeable future.

But now death was here. Soon it would come rushing after her. As soon as Steiner appeared, she must crawl deeper into the willow thicket.

There was a figure in the yard between the buildings.

Ken!

It was Ken!

Relief poured over Anna. It was over! It was all over! Ken had managed it! Ken had managed everything!

She fought her way through the willows, not noticing how they tore and hit her as she forced her way forward, and began running up the slope towards Ken.

'Ken,' she called. 'We're here! Ken, we're here!'

The relief that everything was over made her lose her self-control so that when she reached him, she threw herself into his arms and burst into floods of tears. He patted her on the back and said that it had been easy.

Then Peter came forward with his congratulations and asked Ken how he had pulled it off. Had he succeeded in tricking Steiner with the cigarette lighter?

'It was easy,' said Ken. 'He fell for it right away. He put the cigar in his mouth and pressed the lighter. He fell backwards as if the cigar had exploded in his mouth. Both his eyebrows and his hair were singed. The pistol lay unguarded on the table where he had been sitting. I grabbed it. When Steiner rushed at me, I fired. The bullet went right into his heart. He died instantly.'

'Oh, Ken, how awful,' cried Anna. She felt as if she would never be able to stop crying.

20

Hᴇ ᴘᴀᴜsᴇᴅ ᴡʜɪʟᴇ climbing and surveyed the landscape which spread out more and more, the higher he reached. He saw the snow-capped mountains in the west rise in all their majesty. His eyes followed the river from the expansive mirror of the reservoir, where it originated, to the third narrow canyon at the foot of Lektivagge, where it disappeared.

Yesterday this landscape had been an innocent idyll, paradise for people seeking peace in the virgin wilderness. Today it was a battlefield strewn with human corpses. Five dead. He himself had taken the life of one of these. It had been so easy. Steiner had not even had time to be surprised.

The dam looked tiny and vulnerable from up here. He thought that a better place could hardly have been chosen for an assassination. An explosion would instantly release the reservoir's masses of water. The river would be transformed into a flood that would destroy everything in its path.

Ken was worried. Where were Haseke and Sabine hiding out? Why had they not waited up on top until he had come out of the house and given the signal as they had agreed? Haseke had told Peter that he planned to get himself and Sabine out of danger. What had he meant by that? Ken felt obliged to climb up to the high plateau to get a clear idea of what was going on. What was Haseke up to now?

By the pool below the cottages he saw Anna and Peter, no larger than punctuation marks. Peter stood out in the water; Anna seemed to be sitting on the shore. Peter was fishing. Ken had asked them to wait while he climbed the cliff to see where Haseke and Sabine had gone. Of course, Peter had to take the opportunity to fish. That man was not normal. Ken continued climbing upwards. The slope was not hard to ascend; the hardest part was an area of huge boulders which could easily start moving. He walked uphill mostly through low-growing shrubs.

He had misjudged Haseke. Not his skill in battle. His courage, strength and initiative were obvious. But he had believed that Haseke had the same Achilles' heel as so many others of his generation: gentlemanliness. He had thought that Haseke adhered to a code of chivalry, loyalty to one's word and the myth of fair play. He had been mistaken. Just like that, Haseke had broken his promise to wait at the top of the slope.

Why?

Ken checked the pistol that was in his belt, Steiner's pistol. It was fully loaded and cocked. Perhaps Haseke lay behind a cliff, waiting for him. He was prepared for all eventualities. He was not taking the risk of underestimating Haseke once again.

Ken caught sight of them when he had climbed the slope and reached the plateau—two tiny figures way out in the distance of this mountain landscape. More than ten kilometres away, he estimated. He stopped. Pursuit was pointless. He wondered why Haseke had abandoned the appointed place. Probably he was sure that Steiner would win the duel in the cottage and then set out to hunt himself and Sabine. The old warrior had fled with his girl under his arm and his tail between his legs.

Ken wondered if Haseke would try to reach civilization, or if he planned to pitch camp at a safe distance from the centre of the action, wait for its resolution and the rescue party from the coast which would follow the explosion, and only then reveal himself. Not that it mattered. The main thing was that he was out of the way for the next few hours.

When Ken was halfway down, he took a rest. Peter still stood out in the river fishing. Anna still sat on the shore. It was too bad about Anna. She was his type of woman, bold, honest and also warm and feminine. He remembered the abandon with which they had made love. He remembered the cool warmth of her body, the suppleness, the strength. For an instant it crossed his mind to throw it all in, take her with him to some secluded place in some secluded country where they could love, have children and live a life just like everybody else.

He continued his descent and concentrated his thoughts on what he had to do. Thinking ahead was a means of sustaining one's energy. Thinking back was something for old-age pensioners, priests and philosophers. An active person must think ahead. About the next move in the game.

'Did you see them anywhere?' asked Anna when he came down to the river and approached her. She had red marks all over her face as if she had been beaten, her skin was covered with mosquito bites, her hair was matted and oily from the mosquito repellent.

'They're making an expedition into the unknown. I'm sure they thought Steiner had killed me and they wanted to put as much distance between them and him as possible.'

'What a mistake!'

'Don't be so sure!'

Anna stared uncomprehendingly at him. A little farther down the shore Peter stood with his fishing rod in his hand. He was dripping wet. He must have tumbled over into the river, poor fellow.

'What exactly do you mean?' asked Anna.

'I think it would have been an even bigger mistake for them to stay.'

Anna looked just as bewildered as he had expected. Peter seemed occupied with his fishing.

'Just how gullible can you be?' he continued, feeling bitter that he was now forced to take action, with everything it involved.

'What?'

'How naïve you've all been, you Clausewitz admirers. You haven't even followed Clausewitz's first rule: never underestimate your enemy. You should have followed it. Then you would never have assumed that your enemy was foolish enough to go into action without reserves. You made a mistake in thinking that Moll and Steiner were the entire force. You should have been more perceptive.'

Anna looked at him searchingly. Then she turned her eyes towards the cottages, next towards the dam and last of all back to Ken.

'You aren't serious?' she said.

'This isn't a joke. I understand that you're surprised. The old joker Ken is suddenly showing his serious side. A very serious side. Deadly serious, one might say.'

Anna kept silent and stared at him. Peter seemed paralysed.

'At seven o'clock tonight this dam is going to blow sky-high. It's my job to make sure that the explosion takes place, now that the others are out of the game. I'd hoped to avoid intervening. You yourself saw how I tried to stop those mad fighting cocks, the major and Haseke. If they'd only stayed out of the way, then

Steiner and Moll could have blown up the dam in peace, and I could have lain low, and you would have been able to return to Stockholm and make a thrilling report with exciting photographs.'

'I can't believe that,' said Anna without conviction.

'In this country you only believe what your eyes see and your ears hear. I'll never forget how I was received the first time I set foot in Sweden. I'm an American deserter, I said. I've deserted my post in Kaiserslautern, and I don't want to be sent to Vietnam again. I've been at the front there for two years already. They fell for everything I said. I was amazed, although I'd been specially trained. I'd learned lots about the Swedish mentality and how deserters behaved; I'd even suffered through four months in the barracks at Kaiserslautern and they believed me without batting an eyelid, probably just because I had hash in my pockets. No one's more gullible than a Swede. During all these years no one has questioned that I am what I claim to be. It's never occurred to anyone that the American secret service might smuggle in a fake deserter to keep tabs on the real ones. Not even to the fellows on the *Express* and *Aftonblad* newspapers.'

'Not to me,' said Anna. 'But it's obvious that it's easy to pull the wool over my eyes. And you must be an expert at tricking people.'

'It's my job. I do what my superiors order me to do. If they say: go to Sweden, pretend to be a deserter, and then report regularly about the state of the American deserters in the country, then I do it. If they say: train to be a photographer, apply for Swedish citizenship, blend into the Swedish community, then I do that too. And if I'm ordered to go up into the Swedish mountains to see to it that an assassination attempt is successfully carried through, then, of course, I obey orders. I'm serving my country.'

'It's a funny way to serve your country,' said Anna. 'Killing your own senator.'

'It's not for me to judge. But I assume that my superiors know what they're doing. Senator Stockwell is considered a threat to our security. He purposefully undermines the American people's fighting spirit and the will to defend. That's the only motive I've been given. It's enough for me.'

'But Steiner,' said Anna. 'You shot Steiner. Why did you do that, if you were both on the same side?'

'I didn't shoot Steiner. The shot went off when I killed him with my hands. He was going to be sacrificed in any case. Both he and Moll. Besides, he wouldn't give me the pistol willingly. He didn't trust me, wouldn't take any risks, was scared after Moll's death and the shoot-out with Haseke. He sensed that something was happening which he couldn't control. He was right. Steiner's and Moll's real mission was never to blow up the dam, but just to seize the cottages and prepare for the explosion. After that, they were to be liquidated. The original plan was as follows: Steiner and Moll were to force you up the cliff where you would sit in the best places to observe the finale, without disturbing a hair on your heads. I alone was to accompany them to the dam. They knew me very well. I was the one who enlisted them in Malmö. But naturally they didn't know that I was to kill them up at the dam. Steiner was to remain behind as the scapegoat. Moll would disappear in the explosion. That's why the police would think that the man later spotted in the Norwegian mountains was Moll. In reality, it would have been me. My escape route is through the Norwegian mountains. While Sweden mourns me among the victims of the catastrophe, I'll withdraw after having completed my mission.'

'And Steiner and Moll will carry the blame alone.'

'Of course! They can be traced to their lodgings in Malmö. There's suitable identification awaiting discovery there. Probably some poor shady organization in the East will take the blame for the whole thing.'

'Unbelievable,' said Anna. 'To think that charming Ken, the fashionable photographer, darling of all the girls, now reveals himself to be a secret agent. They'll never believe me when I tell them at the office. They'll only laugh. They'll say it's a new amusing invention of the far left. Although, it's obvious, I won't be seeing the office again.'

Ken thought it was too bad that Anna looked so afraid. Frightened women were never pretty. Beauty is the result of self-assurance; the presentation of assets in which one has confidence. Here you are, help yourself. Anna was pale under the red streaks and blotches on her face. Her mouth colourless. Her eyes blank.

'I'm sorry that you were the one who came here with me,' said Ken. 'If I'd known you when I chose you, then I would have chosen someone else. The witness to my real identity isn't so lucky.'

'Presumably that's supposed to be a compliment. Do you usually compliment your victims before you kill them? I suspect that you're planning to shoot me with that pistol you have in your hand.'

'I'd rather avoid the shooting. I thought you and Peter could follow me up to the guest cottage. I know a good place to lock you in. The end is the same in any case. No one will survive the flood.'

'There won't be any flood!'

It was Peter who suddenly was speaking. The words came out of his mouth unevenly as if his tongue were untied all at once. Ken thought Peter looked foolish standing there on the shore dripping wet and with a fishing rod in his hand. Ken noticed that he was not using a reel but had the line tied right to the handle. The line drooped pathetically in the water. The incompetent fool.

'What did you say?' Ken laughed.

'I said there won't be any flood.'

'Is that so? Why's that?'

'For lack of explosives.' Peter spoke so quietly that Ken could barely hear him. His whole body trembled. He seemed terrified.

'Wrong,' said Ken. 'I have access to thirty kilos of explosives just as the major calculated. That's more than enough.'

'I've suspected that you were collaborating with Steiner and Moll for a long time,' said Peter.

'Bullshit!'

'Yes!'

'Since when?'

'Since I helped Moll carry the major out of the kitchen. The floor was soaking wet. Used matches were floating in the liquid. It was obvious that the major had poured out the contents of the petrol can and tried to set it alight. But the liquid on the floor wasn't petrol. Someone had dumped the petrol and replaced it with water. It couldn't have been anyone but you.'

'Why not?'

'Steiner and Moll are eliminated. They didn't know what was

happening. It couldn't have been Anna because she's a victim of events the same as I am. Haseke and the major were involved in the attack. That only leaves you!'

'He must have been very baffled, the old warrior,' said Ken. 'Standing there, waiting for an explosion while the matches only hissed and died.'

'But there was another thing that made me sure that you weren't what you pretended to be, that you were collaborating with Steiner and Moll.'

'What was that?'

'The cigarette lighter.'

'Didn't you see its shooting flame?' said Ken.

'Yes, but Steiner never did. He was one of those snobbish smokers who always light their cigars according to the strictest rules of the art. He held the cigar between his thumb and index finger and moved it slowly into the flame of a match. He would never have dreamed of holding the cigar in his mouth when he lit it. You could never have tricked him into doing that. I noticed it for the first time during the lecture about the fishing at breakfast yesterday.'

'What do you know! Yes, well, maybe it would have failed. How do I know? I never tried it; it was completely unnecessary. When he didn't want to give me the pistol willingly, I just bided my time until he turned his back on me. He wasn't expecting an attack from me, so it was child's play. You aren't as stupid as you look, Peter. Excellent conclusions. There's only one thing I don't understand. If you were convinced that I was collaborating with Steiner and Moll, why didn't you do something about it?'

'But I did.'

'Pardon?' For the first time Ken felt a crack in his self-confidence. Was it possible that this wretch had put a spoke in his wheel?

'That's what I've been trying to tell you. You don't have any explosives any more. I found them and took them away from you.'

'Bullshit! Where did you find them?'

'Ask rather what I did with them.'

Peter pointed at a spot beyond the Table Rock, just about where Haseke and Moll had tumbled into the water a few hours ago.

'There,' he said. 'I went out on to the rock and dumped everything into the water. They're ruined by now.'

Ken controlled himself with great effort. What had happened? This coward, had he really ruined everything? He could not believe it. Wait! Water did not damage gelignite!

'Where did you heave it?' Ken asked calmly, pointing the pistol at Peter. Where exactly?'

'There!' Peter pointed once again. 'Directly beyond the Table Rock.'

Ken walked past Anna, where she sat on the shore, and went out on to the Table Rock. He stopped and pointed the pistol at Peter. Then at Anna.

'Don't try any tricks,' he said. 'I'm not as easily fooled as Moll was.'

Step by step he went out to the tip of the Table Rock. The whole time with the pistol ready to shoot.

He looked down into the swirling water. He could not see a thing. He looked back at Peter and Anna. Peter raised the tip of his rod as if he'd had a bite; Anna moved to a rock along the water's edge. He had them under control. He peered down into the water again.

Suddenly he saw a nylon line coming up out of the water just by the Table Rock. He heard a rustling behind him and saw the nylon line approaching over the stones.

Then he understood—a snare!

On the shore Peter thrust the rod backwards. Ken tried to shoot, but the snare tightened around his legs and he lost his balance. His feet were pulled out from under him. He hit the rocks with his back and elbows, was tugged out over the edge, drawn into the water.

Peter pulled with all his might. The pressure on the rod grew enormous as Ken's body glided into the mainstream. Triumph swelled within him as, slowly but surely, it glided into the middle of the river. This was exactly as he had planned it. The current would carry Ken over to the opposite side.

Ken came closer and closer to the shoreline. He washed ashore on his back, turned over, and freed himself from the snare around his wrists. Then he collapsed there.

'Jesus!' said Anna. 'He still has the pistol!'

Peter saw it too. Ken was still clutching it in his right hand. That was a mistake. 'Come,' said Peter to Anna. 'We've got to get out of range before he comes to.'

They began to walk up to the cottages. Peter felt unburdened as if he had just removed a heavy backpack which he had been carrying for a long time. He had been right about Ken. He had suspected him for a long time. Not only had he suspected him of substituting the major's petrol with water, but also for bluffing about the lighter trick. He had suspected his whole attitude; right from the start, he had had a feeling that Ken's philosophy of non-violence was a fraud. It was Ken's complete about-turn, when he offered himself as a hostage for Steiner, that changed his suspicion into conviction. The committed pacifist had become a committed activist all too quickly.

But Anna had refused to believe that Ken was collaborating with Steiner and Moll to blast the dam, or that he was anything other than her assistant photographer; even less, did she believe that Ken was planning to kill her. None of Peter's arguments had convinced her that they ought to lay a trap for Ken. Peter had had to set the trap on his own.

It was this plan that made him come alive. It was dangerous, but it was far more dangerous to do nothing at all. During the past few years he had lived with the feeling that life itself was a trap from which there was no escape. He had carried this feeling with him everywhere. But now, when his worst nightmares about life had become reality and while he was waiting to be brutally murdered, he had suddenly found a way out. It was as if strength had been building up inside him during these years of passivity, and now all at once it was at his disposal.

He had taken his rod and attached a strong nylon line and heavy spinner to it. Then he had cast the spinner over to the opposite shore and hooked it there securely. Without hesitation, he had gone out into the water, and holding the rod pulled himself over to the other shore. There, he first cast the spinner back to the shore he had just come from, then fastened the reel to a steady rock, let the line loose so that the reel would work as a pulley, and holding the end of the line in his hand, had pulled himself back to the other shore again.

Dripping wet, he stood there holding both ends of the line. He put one end through the guides of the rod and attached it to the handle. The other, he tied into a snare, which he placed out around the rock slab. He let the snare's knot catch under the rock so that the force of the current would not pull it towards the line across the river.

All that remained was the bluff about the explosives. It had been perfect even though Peter had not had the slightest idea of where the gelignite was hidden.

Halfway to the cottage, he turned around. Ken had got up into a sitting position.

'What do we do now?' asked Anna.

'We must try to reach the other cottage and warn the senator. I'm sure he will start to pursue us. But at seven o'clock he must set off the explosion at the dam. That means he must break off the chase so that he's back at the cottages by six thirty at the latest.' Peter looked at his watch. 'Two minutes to one,' he said. 'He can start the pursuit from the cottages at about two o'clock. That gives him four and a half hours before he has to be back here again. In other words he has to turn back at quarter past four.'

They had reached the cottages when Anna turned round. Ken had started upstream along the narrow shore under the cliff wall. He was running. Anna also started running. Peter dashed after her, and grabbed her arm to hold her back. 'Take it easy. We won't gain anything by rushing off.'

'But he'll catch us up!'

Anna tried to shake herself free from his grip. He saw the panic in her eyes.

'This race won't be won by speed, but by staying power and sound judgment. We need shoes on our feet and we need some provisions.'

'Let me go!' screamed Anna. She tugged and pulled to get free. Peter took her by both arms and shook her like a child.

'Calm down, Anna,' he said. She began to cry. He drew her to him and held her in his arms. 'Whether it's fear or confidence,' he said, 'it's as if you and I were sitting on either end of a seesaw. When one end goes up, the other goes down. Let's both slide in towards the middle and get through this together.'

21

P ETER FIRST CAUGHT sight of him when he emerged from the birch woods down by the deserted hut. At such a great distance he looked like an insect, eager, inexhaustible and completely without leniency.

He looked at his watch. It was two thirty. Ken's progress followed his estimate. They'd been at the same spot at quarter to two. That is forty-five minutes ago. Their lead had diminished.

He had chosen the resting place with great care: on top of a precipice where the old trail wound up the cliff from the deserted hut down in the valley. He sat so that he could see everything that happened on the trail, yet he was still hidden. Anna lay on her back in the high grass with her eyes closed. This last difficult ascent had used all her strength. When they stopped and he brought out the food, she had put away the four cheese sandwiches he had made for her and drunk two cups of water from a mountain stream nearby. Now he was breathing evenly and quietly.

'Those five minutes are up. Time to get going!' Peter helped Anna to her feet.

'How do you feel?'

'Better. At least there aren't any mosquitoes here.' They began to follow the trail.

Ahead of them was a wide plateau. Up here there were no trees that could throw a shadow. Only shrubs grew here: dwarf birch, crowberries, blueberries and heather, which glowed red and yellow in the autumn but had not yet turned these colours. A gentle wind was blowing from the south. It cooled them down and dried the sweat off their faces. Large cotton wads of white clouds flocked over the white-crested mountains in the west.

The trail was almost completely overgrown but Peter had followed abandoned trails before and could also follow this one with the help of the gaps in vegetation which were still left. It pointed directly southwards, which perplexed him, because the pass they had to cross over behind Lektivagge lay almost directly east. But he did not take a short-cut. He knew that there were rarely short-cuts in the mountains. If a trail seemed to make an inexplicable bend, which one tried to eliminate by taking a short-cut, sooner or later one ended up in a bog or by a creek one could not wade across.

The only possible route to the lodge where the senator was went over the pass. He estimated that Lektivagge was more than fifteen hundred metres high and that the pass was between eleven and twelve hundred metres. From the height they were now at there was still an ascent of another three hundred metres. But there were still many kilometres before the ascent began.

Anna went first. So far she had held a good pace. Peter wondered how long it would last. He himself felt strong and free. He wondered if his strength would also be enough for Anna.

Lemmings were swarming everywhere. It had been a good summer for the lemmings; they would probably start their death-migration later that autumn. Most of them ran away rustling through the scrub, frightened by the steps of the two walkers. But there were a few who did not move, probably those who lived nearest the path. They took defensive positions with bared teeth and loud hisses. Despite their tremendous inferiority, they did not give up; they chose to stay and fight.

Anna stopped. She could not see the path any more. Peter had pointed it out to her but now it had disappeared. She seemed more tired now.

'It veers to the left here,' said Peter.

'You go first.'

Peter started down the path, which had nearly completely disappeared under the dwarf birch thicket. Now it went directly east. Now and again he turned his head and glanced to where the trail reached the plateau. Still not a glimpse of Ken. Behind his back he could hear Anna's breathing growing heavier and heavier. Ahead of them lay the high pass.

When they reached the beginning of the ascent Anna was very tired. Peter stopped by the side of a stream which, calm and idyllic, came running down from the pass. It was clear that the path followed the stream.

'We'll have a rest here,' said Peter.

Anna sank down on to a lush tuft of grass by the stream and Peter gave her water to drink.

'Look,' said Anna suddenly. 'Ken!'

Peter turned his head. Ken had reached a point well out on the plateau behind them.

He looked at his watch. Five past three. Ken was gaining on them slowly but surely. He gained about twenty minutes every hour. Would he catch up with them?

The problem reminded him of childhood sums about A and B who rowed, drove a car or sawed at different rates. Now A and B were out walking. Both started from the same spot but B started an hour later than A. However B walked faster than A. He gained twenty minutes on A every hour. How long would it take before B caught up with A?

Answer: B catches up with A in three hours.

Ken would reach them at about four o'clock.

'Let's go now,' said Peter.

They followed alongside the stream through a bed of soft grass, while they each chewed a chocolate biscuit that Peter had pulled out of his pocket. On their left the slope which formed the south side of Lektivagge was smooth and rounded. The mountain on their right was steep and inaccessible.

The incline grew steeper and steeper, the rock barer and barer. Still they walked on soft grass alongside the stream but it grew sparser the higher they climbed. They had to make a detour around a steel-grey rock. Anna's breath sounded heavier and heavier behind Peter's back.

He turned around. Ken had come far, nearly up to their resting place down by the stream. He was gaining on them faster than Peter had estimated. He made a new calculation. Ken would have caught up with them by ten to four. That gave Ken quite enough time to fire two shots before he had to turn back.

'He's catching up with us,' said Anna.

'Can you speed up?'

'I don't have the energy; I'm dead tired.'

They followed the stream upwards until it disappeared underneath a section of steep boulders. A rushing and rippling sound under the rocks revealed where it flowed. Climbing over those rugged rocks had taxed their strength. Anna stopped.

'I can't go on any longer. You continue.'

'Not alone.'

'Don't be foolish! What's the point of our both being shot?

You could get away on your own. You could warn the senator!'

'Now then! Let's continue.'

'It won't work.'

'It will. We'll just climb up this precipice here. Then we'll act like the lemmings. We'll stop and fight.'

'You're crazy!'

Peter took her arm and dragged her up the precipice. He had no idea how this plan of stopping and fighting would work. He only knew that he would never give in or abandon Anna. For many years he had felt as if he were an ant faced with thundering footsteps approaching him. Now he had rid himself of his fears. He would never give up hope again.

At last they reached the top of the precipice. Anna held herself up with Peter's arm. The path levelled out and they lost sight of Ken. He would not be able to see them until he had climbed the precipice.

The stream emerged into the daylight and the path followed alongside it into a valley on the right. Then the stream made an abrupt right-angle to the left where the path began again above the next precipice. Inside its angle a smaller stream plunged headlong through a narrow ravine with sharp rocks on either side.

Peter looked at his watch. Three thirty. It would take about fifteen minutes for Ken to reach the top of the precipice. They would be out of sight in fifteen minutes. Peter had an idea.

'Hurry up, Anna,' he said.

He pointed at the little ravine in the corner of the mountain wall in front of them.

'We'll climb up there. Do you see that rock ledge up there?'

He raised his hand and pointed at a protruding rock by the side of the ravine, about twenty metres above the path. On its flat surface two people could lie hidden from discovery from below.

'I'll never make it. It's too steep.'

'I'll help you. It's our only chance.'

Anna had recovered a little on the flat ground up to the ravine. They stopped where the small brook tumbled into the larger one.

'Just pretend this ravine is a staircase,' said Peter. 'Admittedly, the steps are a bit uneven, but we can walk up them. Remember two rules: first of all, climb in an upright position. Don't lean inwards, or you'll get off balance. Secondly, always have a good hold with three of your hands and feet while you're seeking a hold for the fourth.'

They started climbing. Peter coaxed Anna upwards, bit by bit. He pointed out suitable footholds, warned her about loose stones and boosted her from below when the strength in her leg muscles gave way, or pulled her upwards with a tight grip around her wrists.

The ravine was steep but not especially difficult to climb. Peter realized that it would be assigned a three on the scale of mountain climbing which rated all ascents with a number from one to six. Pitons and ropes would have been a help but were not necessary. The greatest difficulty was the water splashing from the brook which washed down on their left. It made the rocks wet and slippery and also increased their feeling of pursuit and anxiety.

Yet the climbing went faster than Peter had expected. When he had pulled Anna up on to the rock ledge, they still had a few minutes left before Ken would arrive. The ledge was like a shelf on the mountain wall. The surface was as large as a normal dining-room table—and it even had flowers growing between some loose stones. Peter noticed a glacier crowfoot. Then he counted the stones. There were six. All about the same size, like large cabbages or cannon balls.

Peter rolled two of the stones over the edge. He placed them as far out as possible, leaving a narrow slit between them through which he could look down into the valley without being seen. Then he told Anna to lie down right next to the mountain wall. He lay down full length behind the stones, looking down at the top of the precipice.

Ken appeared. First his blond hair and broad shoulders, then his whole body was over the top. He had climbed quickly and gained still more time. Peter looked at his watch. Seventeen minutes to four. Ken was half running in the valley below them. His heavy breathing was not exhausted, feeble panting but an athlete's practised technique for supplying the body with oxygen. His haste pleased Peter: for one thing it proved that Ken really was in a hurry and that Peter's conclusion that Ken would have to turn back soon was correct; and it also forced Ken to keep his eyes focused on the ground.

Ken passed directly below them while they lay as motionless as two forgotten objects on a hat rack. He did not look up. He continued tirelessly up the new ascent which led towards the highest point of the pass. He was no longer the charming photographer, joking his way through his surroundings. He was the ruthless hunter stalking his prey. Good, thought Peter. This concentration on his goal might keep Ken on the track long enough.

Peter turned to Anna. She lay on her stomach with her face in the glacier crowfoot looking at him intently. He motioned with his thumb and she nodded in reply. He wondered if she had perceived the direction of his plan. Their rock ledge lay at a lower level than the highest part of the pass to which Ken was heading. When he reached there, he would probably notice that there was no one fleeing ahead of him. Then he would stop and turn round. Where are they hiding, he would ask himself. From up there he would spot them as easily as a hawk spies a bird's nest in a mountain crevice. They could do nothing to hide themselves. The ravine where the brook flowed was also open to view from above. They could only hope for luck.

Ken continued heading towards the blue sky above the top of the pass. His progress was slower on this abrupt ascent, which was so steep that now and again he had to use his hands. When he reached the top, he stopped. He raised his hand and shaded his eyes as if he could not believe what he saw.

Peter looked at his watch. Five to four. No matter how it went he had made Ken lose many minutes.

Ken turned around sharply. He spotted them within two seconds. He stuck his hand in his pocket, drew out the pistol, aimed at them and fired. The shot echoed between the mountain walls. It did not hit. That could not have been its intention either because the distance between them was four or five hundred metres.

Ken rushed down the slope as if he were the one being pursued. He leapt and bounded, slipped and skidded, fell and got up again. The whole time with the pistol in his hand.

When he reached the ravine he waded across the larger stream and began climbing the rocks of the ravine. He chose the same route as Peter had chosen. But he climbed more quickly. He would reach them within a couple of minutes.

If he were not stopped.

Peter put his hand on one of the two stones shielding him. He gave it a push. It rolled over the edge of the cliff and fell into the ravine with a crash.

The noise warned Ken.

He pressed himself in towards the mountainside and avoided being hit by the rock by a few centimetres. He drew his pistol and aimed; and Peter barely managed to pull back his head before the shot went off.

Peter lay still and counted to fifty. He must let Ken start climbing again. Then he shoved the second stone. He heard it thundering down through the ravine and finally landing in the brook with a smash.

Had it hit?

He did not dare look down to see. He crawled towards Anna, pulled loose two of the remaining stones of their shelter and rolled them towards the edge. He put them next to each other and peered down.

He saw Ken raise his pistol. The shot hit the left stone with a bang, deafening him. He pushed the stone and it set off with the same din as before.

Before the shot he had managed to see that Ken had only reached a metre further on from the place he had been when the first stone fell.

He gave the second stone a shove. Then he crawled back and brought out the last two stones. He lay quietly behind them and counted to one hundred. Then he peered forward. Ken was on his way upwards again. He pushed against one of the remaining stones and watched it bouncing down the cliffs below. It struck the rock above Ken with a crash like a cannon shot and described a wide curve through the air until it landed with a dull thud in the grass by the edge of the brook.

Ken shot.

The bullet hit the cliff wall above Anna so that the rock shattered and a shower of gravel fell down on her.

'Jesus,' she whispered.

'Just lie still,' Peter ordered.

He was surprised at how calm he was. There was one stone left with which to bombard Ken. Besides himself. He had decided that as a last defensive measure he would hurl himself at Ken and drag him down on to the cliffs with himself. He stood a greater chance of surviving such a fall than Ken did. Although the chance was minimal.

He looked at his watch. It was ten past four. He shoved the last stone over the edge. When the rumbling had ceased, he heard the rustling of hasty movements in the ravine. He looked down.

Ken was moving rapidly.

Downwards.

Ken had given up.

Peter turned on to his back and looked up at the blue sky. A golden eagle with a vast wingspan soared high above like a symbol of his boundless relief.

They had won.

22

O N T H E O T H E R side of the pass the terrain was different. The high mountains were undulating and sloped gradually down towards the forest far in the east. There began the foothills, rounded and hilly like human heads with bald pates and well trimmed tonsures of birchwoods around the sides.

The trail twisted in wide curves around the rocks and precipices but Peter could still make out its main direction. It pointed towards the nearest spur of the light green strip of forest. He gathered that the river emerged from its canyon there and once again flowed through an open valley. There lay the goal of their expedition: the fishing lodge with its valuable contents, Senator Stockwell.

Anna seemed tired again. They had walked for an hour and a half with just a short break since leaving the rock ledge and starting on the trail again. But Peter had first gone down to the top of the precipice. He could not resist the pleasure of seeing Ken returning unsuccessfully from his mission.

Peter was worried about Anna. How close was she to the limit of her endurance? He was surprised that she still dragged herself onwards. He had seen big strong men collapse on less strenuous mountain hikes from lack of experience. The wilderness placed a set of demands on its visitors completely different from the daily exertions of city life.

In the beginning Anna had been able to keep a rapid pace. The rest on the rock ledge had renewed her strength and the descent on the other side of the pass had used different muscles from the earlier ascent. But once again Peter could hear her heavy breathing behind his back. When they reached a rapid stream which they had to cross, he raised his hand.

'We'll stop for five minutes,' he said. 'It's always best to take a break before fording a stream so that one's rested when one gets across.'

Anna's face was white under her sunburn. She looked as if she would need to recover for at least a week. She collapsed on the soft grass. Peter bent over the crystal-clear water. His back ached, which was the first sign that this long expedition was beginning to tax him. He cut a piece of cheese and a slice of sausage.

'I'm not hungry,' said Anna.

'Eat.'

She took the piece of cheese he gave her and began chewing mechanically and reluctantly as if it were old chewing-gum.

'What time is it?' she asked.

'Quarter to six.'

'How far do we have left?'

'About seven or eight kilometres.'

'Will we make it?'

'If you eat properly.'

'Why don't you go on alone? I'm fine here. If you have to drag me along, you won't make it in time.'

Peter shook his head.

'It's not worth talking about,' he said. 'The answer is no. You wanted me to abandon you when Ken was pursuing us. I didn't do it then. I won't do it now.'

'You could come back and get me.'

Peter knew she was probably right. The most sensible thing to do would be to hurry ahead and warn the senator as quickly as possible. But he could not. He felt that if he let her out of his sight for a second, he would lose her for ever. He realized that the feeling was foolish. But it still gripped him in the same way his fear had earlier. However, the difference was enormous: the fear had been his enemy, his feeling for Anna was his best friend.

'No,' he said.

Anna looked out at the water rushing past.

'I haven't thanked you yet for saving my life,' she said softly.

'Don't do it, either,' he said. 'In fact, it's quite the reverse. You're the one who saved my life.'

Anna smiled.

'In that case we have something in common,' she said.

'Then you understand why I can't leave you alone here in the mountains.'

Anna stuffed in the rest of the cheese and chewed like an obedient girl. Then she bit into the piece of sausage and succeeded in getting it down with the help of a mug full of water.

'I'm ready,' she said, and stood up.

They crossed the stream with the water rushing up to their knees and continued walking down the mountain. After a few hundred metres Peter noticed that exhaustion was already beginning to overcome Anna again. She complained about blisters on her feet and muscle cramps. The worst was that her legs would not carry her. He had to support her. Still she stumbled frequently and nearly fell.

At six thirty Peter had to let Anna rest again. There were still one and a half kilometres before they reached the stream. After a few minutes he got her going again. He put her left hand around his neck, held her with a firm grip around the waist and half carried, half pushed her forward.

It was ten to seven when they reached the edge of the plateau. They looked down into the river's canyon where it widened into a green valley of gushing water, flowering meadows, deep willow thickets and groves of white-trunked birch. The perfect location for an exclusive fishing lodge.

Only Peter could not see it.

'There's no lodge there,' said Anna.

Peter followed the beautiful winding river with his eyes. There it lay. Half-hidden by a hill and nearly completely obscured by spreading birches.

'It's down there,' he said pointing. 'That's it. It must be almost a kilometre away.'

'All that for nothing.'

That was exactly what Peter was thinking. Still he did not want to give up.

'We'll keep going. Perhaps Ken won't explode the dam on time. Maybe something's happened to delay him.'

'Yes,' said Anna.

They continued along the rim of the steep slope down towards the valley. Peter looked for signs of life and activity down there. Perhaps he would see the senator or someone else down by the river engaged in the evening's fishing. The time was perfect, the sun had just recently deserted the bottom of the valley.

But there was no one to be seen. Well, they could be anywhere, behind a hill, behind some of the thick willows, behind one of the birch groves. Perhaps they were at one of the fishing spots farther downstream. Peter quickened his pace.

Then Anna fell. Suddenly she lay headlong in the heather as if her legs had been pulled out from under her, motionless as if she never planned to get up again.

Peter looked at his watch. Five to seven.

He fell to his knees beside her and shook her shoulder.

'Anna,' he said. 'Anna!'

He noticed a spot of dirt on her cheek. Carefully he wiped it away. She opened her eyes and looked at him.

'I must have fallen,' she said quietly.

Peter picked her up. She was light. Once again he wound her left arm around his neck, gripping her wrist firmly at the same time as he supported her around the waist. They started moving forward again.

Now the lodge became completely visible; they had come so far that it was no longer hidden by the hill or birches. It was the same barrack-like structure as the cottage in which they had been staying. An open window and some white garden furniture indicated that the lodge was occupied. A faint wisp of smoke rose from the chimney. But there was no one in sight. Everyone must be fishing farther along the river.

Peter looked at his watch. Two minutes left.

He stopped.

'We could start our descent here,' he said. They were directly above the cottage.

Anna did not answer. She just clung to him and breathed heavily. Peter bent his knees slowly and let Anna sit down on the ground. He knew well that he could not take her down the cliff before she had rested and regained her strength.

'What time is it?' asked Anna.

Peter checked.

'One minute to seven.'

'You're not planning to climb down, are you?'

'No.'

Peter sat down next to Anna on the edge of the cliff. There was nothing he could do. To go down into the valley was suicide. He looked up and down the visible parts of the river's shoreline but still could see no one. Everything down there suggested peace and innocent quiet. The river flowed, sparkling and beautiful, between the gentle shore lines. Trees and bushes blazed with greenery, flowers blossomed in competition with each other in the mountain meadow. Somewhere in this scenery there was a handful of people enjoying the countryside without a clue that within a couple of seconds this idyll would be transformed into a raging death-trap.

Peter looked at his watch.

'Ten seconds left,' he said.

They sat silently next to each other, waiting for the sound of the explosion from the west. There was no bird to be seen, no breath of wind; nature seemed to hold its breath.

'Now,' said Peter.

It was exactly seven.

They both stared at the high Lektivagge Mountain behind whose rugged mass Paktasjaure was hidden. And the dam.

Nothing happened.

'Is your watch accurate?'

'Yes, within a few seconds.'

They were quiet and concentrated on waiting. There was no

sound except the calming roar of the river. A pair of ptarmigan flew up out of the willows below them as if the waiting had become too much for them. Peter noticed how Anna jumped when the silence was broken by the beating of their wings. He gazed at the birds. They flew across the river and landed in the shrubbery on the other shore.

Still no explosion.

'One minute past,' said Peter.

'Something must have gone wrong,' said Anna.

They were silent again. Peter followed the second hand on its way around the clockface with his eyes. Second led to second, minute to minute. Nothing happened.

'Look!' Anna pointed near the cottage. 'A dog!'

A large Alsatian walked quietly across the yard towards the door. It sat down in front of the step. Peter assumed that this was the warden's dog which had come on ahead to the cottage from somewhere. The dog lay down on its side as if it were preparing for a long wait ahead.

'What do we do now?' asked Anna.

Peter shrugged his shoulders. Eventually they would have to go down into the valley and contact the people whoever they were.

Then came the explosion.

A dull bang echoed from the mountain in the west. Peter leapt up and looked towards Lektivagge. A faint cloud of smoke rose over the edge of the mountain. Behind it the dam had been blown up.

Silence.

Peter felt Anna clutching his arm. She had also stood up.

Then he heard a low rumble.

At first it sounded like a train in the distance. Then like a tank driving through the bottom of the ravine, approaching nearer and nearer. Flocks of birds rose in a line from the foot of Lektivagge; the line also came nearer and nearer. A white stream of water vapour followed the birds. The low rumble grew into a loud roaring.

Peter tore his eyes away from the drama along the ravine and looked down into the valley. Had the people realized the danger? Were they trying to escape to safety?

There was no sign of anyone.

Except the dog. It sat motionlessly on the ground outside the cottage and listened with its ears pricked up towards the mountain in the west.

'God,' shouted Anna.

Peter looked at the mouth of the ravine where the river flowed out into the valley. The flood was coming. It filled the mouth with a wall of foaming water, surged forward through the ravine and heaved itself over the valley, swallowing everything. Birches were splintered, bushes wrenched up. In full fury the water surged forward towards the cottage. The dog started running. It rushed up the slope in a panic.

The water reached the cottage, knocked it over like a house of cards, and swept the wreckage along with it.

The dog ran for its life. It saw that it would never reach anything high enough, turned and tried to run away from the onrushing wall of water.

It was no use. The water crashed down over the dog and drowned it.

A horrible sight. Peter thought about the senator and the others who were at this moment being knocked over and drowned in the same way as the dog. Down there in that torrent of water, debris and mud.

A cry was heard through the roar of the onsurging water. Barely audible, but still completely distinctive in the way that a human call always distinguishes itself from other sounds.

'Did you hear?' Anna shouted in his ear.

'Someone called,' he shouted back.

'Oh, Jesus!' Anna hid her face in her hands. Peter put his arm around her. A gesture without meaning. The drama was finished. The catastrophe was a fact.

23

A NNA LOOKED OUT over the valley where the flood had been. Everything was ruined and destroyed. Only the river was the same. It flowed calmly in its bed like a wild animal which had spent its fury and now lay down to rest. The cottage was gone. There was not a trace of it left on the place where it had once stood. Not even the place was left. The grass was gone as well as the earth where the grass had grown. The ground was washed away down to the bedrock.

The meadow of flowers was gone. Those willows which had not been uprooted stood leafless as in winter. The groves of birch were broken and washed away. The stumps of their trunks stuck up out of the ground like a forest devastated by war.

The air was full of fluttering and crying birds which had nowhere to go.

Anna thought about the senator. Had he been taken by surprise and killed on the spot or had he tried to flee to safety? And the others? None of them had stood a chance of escaping. She wondered about the call she had heard through the noise of the crushing water. It still rang in her ears.

She wondered what had happened farther down the river where the flood had reached. Had many cottages been swept away? Had many people been crushed and drowned? And what would happen when the flood reached the power station? And then the larger communities along the river towards the sea? Would an even greater catastrophe follow? A national catastrophe?

Peter suddenly raised his hand and listened.

'I thought I heard voices,' he said.

Anna listened. She could only hear the birds' screeching and the river's roar. She glanced down into the valley. What she suddenly saw made her forget her exhaustion.

A man was walking down the slope. He came from a spot at the edge of the plateau about a hundred metres farther on. He was on his way towards the place where the cottage had once stood. He was dressed in a green fishing jacket and green wellingtons.

At the same time she heard voices.

'Fantastic!' said Peter. 'Did you hear? There are people there. They've survived.'

He pointed at the man on the slope.

'Is that the senator?'

'No. But maybe that's the senator!'

She took Peter by the hand and pulled him with her. The voices seemed to be coming from a spot about ten metres down the slope, which lay hidden from them. Anna's legs carried her without difficulty. She wanted to run to the senator and congratulate him on his incredible luck.

'Wait,' said Peter. 'Take it easy.'

'Hurry up! It must be the senator.'

'Yes, but we mustn't rush into it! We've got to take it easy and think for a minute.'

Anna grew impatient with his stubbornness.

'Hello, down there,' she called. 'Hello!'

A head came up over the edge of the cliff. Senator Stockwell. Another popped up next to it. It was Maclean, the security chief. Two pairs of eyes stared in amazement at Anna and Peter. The senator shouted something which they could not understand. He started waving. The security chief waved too. Then they both heaved themselves over the edge of the cliff and began climbing up the slope towards Anna and Peter. Below them, a third man continued on his way to the place where the cottage had once stood.

'Miss Berger!' The senator announced from ten metres' distance that he had recognized her. As always, he looked fresh and neat, as if he had just stepped out of an advert for breakfast cereal—although his facial expression was strained as if he were choking on the cereal.

'How wonderful!' Anna went to meet him. 'I thought you were dead. What a disaster!' She motioned down towards the valley.

Senator Stockwell held out his hand.

'What a terrible thing,' he said. 'What a catastrophe! It's pure chance that we aren't dead! We were on our way to fish in the lake up here on the plateau. If we'd been fishing in the river as usual then ...' He threw open his hands. 'But you, Miss Berger! What are you doing here? In the midst of all this?'

'That's a long story.'

'A dam must have burst.'

'Worse than that! It was blown up on purpose. The flood was meant to drown you and everyone down by the river. How many of you are there?'

'Just Maclean and myself and the Swedish warden.' The senator pointed at the man down by the river. 'He went down to look for his dog. We all survived. What incredible luck! What do you mean, the dam was blown up on purpose? Are you saying it was an assassination attempt? It's not possible.'

'We were there. We stayed in a fishing lodge like the one that was here. There were ten of us, seven men and three women. Two of the men seized the lodge. They killed the housekeeper and the warden and took the rest of us hostage, while they prepared to blast the dam. Then there was a struggle . . .'

Anna fell silent. The events rushed up from the past as if they had been released now that everything was over. A wave of horror surged through her, the dam broke; she surrendered herself to her feelings.

She felt someone take hold of her and let her cry in his arms. She shook with sobs like a child.

In the far distance she heard Peter continue her account of what had happened at Paktas Lodge. He told how the major was killed, how Haseke fought with Moll in the river and then fled with Sabine into the mountains, how Ken revealed his true identity and the role of the two kidnappers, and how he and Anna at last managed to escape from Ken after a desperate chase through the mountains.

When the senator started talking, Anna realized that it was in his arms that she was crying. She could tell how tremendously distressed he was by the tone of his voice when he asked Maclean for his explanation of this ruthless attempt on his life, which had caused all these deaths. And Maclean, in turn, asked Peter about the events and people, especially about Ken.

Anna sat up. Ken was her speciality. Still shaking slightly, while holding back her tears, she took over from Peter and told everything that she knew about Ken, from their first meeting at Svensson and Butler in Stockholm to their last encounter on the slope of Lektivagge.

'Did he say explicitly that he was under orders from the

American secret services?' asked the security chief, when she'd finished.

'Yes.'

'I know that the CIA has infiltrators among our deserters in Canada as well as in Scandinavia. It's obvious that they also have a man in Stockholm. What Miss Berger tells us about Ken fits exactly into the pattern of how the CIA establishes an agent in another country. Especially the fact that they left him alone for a long time to blend into the country where he would later work. Just like capital lying and accumulating interest. The longer you wait, the more he's worth when you really put him into action.'

'I'm sure you're right,' said the senator. 'But it certainly isn't part of the CIA's duty to try to assassinate one of their own country's senators.' He spoke monotonously and uncertainly as if he didn't believe what he was saying, as if he were reciting a memorized lesson which he didn't understand.

'Not the CIA as an organization,' said Maclean. 'But today the CIA is infiltrated by all kinds of outside interests. Both the arms industry and the Pentagon have influence in the CIA. Influence which has pull when persuading an organization official to give the right order to a certain agent, for example, the agent in Stockholm.'

'There's no way they haven't tried to get me,' said the senator quietly.

'And it's typical of the CIA to sweep away all the traces by leading the suspicions in another direction.' said the security chief. 'Neither the Swedish police nor the American public would link the CIA with the attempt. All clues would lead eastward through the two saboteurs, Steiner and Moll.'

He turned to Anna and Peter.

'If it hadn't been for you two . . .' he continued. 'Thanks to you, our enemies will be exposed. The whole world will find out that there are powers in America that will use any means to stop the senator. They're prepared to do anything to prevent him from achieving the aim to which he's dedicated his life: peace and disarmament. They don't mind murder or sabotage. They don't even mind blasting an important dam and creating a natural catastrophe which claims the lives of many people.'

'There's a little snag to all that,' said Peter.

The security chief and the senator looked at him in puzzlement.
'I agree that the assassination attempt had a political aim,' Peter continued. 'But I don't agree about who's behind it. You insist that it's factions within the American military and arms industry.'
'Do you think it's the eastern powers?' asked Maclean impatiently.
'Not at all. I think it's someone completely different.'
Peter leaned towards Maclean.
'I think it's you and the senator.'

24

ANNA LOOKED AT Peter. Perhaps the security chief was right in his judgment of Peter. His caustic answer to Peter's accusation still rang in her ears:
'You must be mad!'
She herself thought that the accusation sounded insane. And Peter expressed it with the same confident certainty which usually characterizes madmen, who think they are Napoleon or Hitler: the greater the certainty, the crazier the ideas.
On the other hand, the whole situation was insane. Being held hostage, the murders, the escape, the explosion of the dam. She looked down on the devastation in the flooded valley. Birds fluttered and screamed in the sky like messengers of death and destruction.
'We must remain calm,' said the senator to Peter. 'Would you be kind enough to explain yourself?'
'The picture that Maclean painted of your role in this assassination attempt is very pretty. Pretty like a tapestry. Only there's a loose thread. If you pull it, the whole tapestry unravels.'
'What's the loose thread?'
'The timing.'

'What do you mean?'

'The time of the explosion was determined beforehand. It was to take place at seven o'clock precisely. This was so important that Ken had to give up chasing Anna and me to get back to carry out the blasting. Why? Why was this so important? There's only one answer to that question: a previously fixed time is used by parties to help them co-ordinate their actions in a plan when they can't communicate with each other. In this case, one party was Ken. I didn't understand who the other party was until I witnessed your miraculous rescue. What made you leave the valley so that you were out of danger exactly when the flood came? Luck? No! Not at all. The only explanation is that you knew that the explosion would take place at seven o'clock. How could you know that? Well, because you yourselves were involved in planning the whole episode.'

'You're tired,' said the senator. 'You've been through some awful experiences. It's taxing on even the strongest people.'

But Anna began to wonder. Could it really be chance that the senator was out of the way when the explosion occurred? She looked at the senator. He met her glance with that complete honesty which only completely honest people can achieve spontaneously. And completely dishonest people after hard training.

'Maybe Ken's superior fixed the time to be sure that the senator was near the river just at that moment,' she said.

'In that case, he would have chosen one in the morning,' said Peter. 'It's dark then, and everyone's in bed.'

'I still can't believe it,' she said.

'It's nice to know I have at least one supporter in the world.' The senator smiled at her.

'This isn't a case of faith,' said Peter, 'but of logic. The previously fixed time for the explosion plus the fact that the senator was out of the danger zone at the same time logically leads to the conclusion that the senator was working with Ken. So many other things do as well. Ken said that he enlisted Steiner and Moll in Malmö for their assignment. He must have known the senator's plans for staying at the fishing lodge owned by the National Board of Crown Forests and Lands well in advance. He must also have known of the existence of the other cottage, Paktas Lodge. And where the dam lay. Where could he have got all this complicated information? The answer's obvious: only from someone who was very close to the senator, who had access to his secret plans. The person lying behind this assassination attempt didn't only control Steiner and Moll. He controlled the whole operation. That's to say, the senator. And who controls the senator? Only himself.'

Suddenly Anna saw that Peter was right. She remembered Ken's sensational photo, the photo which got her involved in this story, the photo of Humlegården park with the senator, the Russian and all the doves. That could not have happened by chance either. It was possible that a photographer might come upon the senator by chance. But not a photographer who had just hired two men to kill the senator. The photo must have been arranged by someone close to the senator.

'Peter,' said Anna. 'It could be Maclean who's behind everything.'

'In that case the senator wouldn't be standing here now. In that case he'd have been down there when the flood came. In that case he'd be dead by now, and Maclean would be the sole survivor.'

'Pardon,' said Maclean. 'Pardon, if I interrupt your interesting speculations about whether I alone am responsible for this attempt on the senator's life, or whether I'm working with the intended victim. Tell me one thing: why the hell would the senator and I want to blow up a dam in Sweden and cause a minor natural disaster?'

'I think you have a political motive. An assassination attempt of this kind would arouse the same tremendous interest as the Watergate scandal. Public sympathy would swing to the senator's side. He'd get a fantastic boost forward.'

'Bullshit.'

'I don't think so. But it isn't my job to understand your motives. The people who investigate this whole affair will do that.'

Anna saw how the security chief was working himself into a rage. His face grew bright red and his chest and shoulders swelled so that he reminded her even more now of that fairytale character she'd thought of the first time she met him: the genie in the bottle.

'What do you mean?' he asked threateningly. 'The police?'
'Of course.'

Peter did not let himself be the least bit intimidated by Maclean's threatening attitude. It struck Anna that only a few hours ago he would have crouched with fright. Peter had undergone a tremendous transformation when he had overcome his fear by the river below Paktas Lodge and had taken up the struggle with Ken. Now he stood calmly when Maclean took a step towards him and hissed in his face:

'I'll never allow that!'

The senator smiled faintly. He reminded Anna of a headmaster arbitrating between two fighting students. He put his hand on Maclean's shoulder.

'George,' he said, 'we've got to take it easy. Very easy. Threats won't get us anywhere. Instead let's retreat while we still can. Let's explain how it all fits together. After all, we're dealing with reasonable young people.'

He turned to Peter.

'You're very level-headed,' he said. 'You're completely right that Maclean and I are behind this entire plan. I take full responsibility. Except for one thing: the bloodshed. If I'd known in advance that innocent people would die, then I would never have approved the plan. I beg you, believe me on that one point.'

The blue eyes glanced at Anna, clear and innocent like a child's. She nodded. She believed him.

'You've also got to believe another thing,' he continued in the same fatherly, appealing tone. 'I'm not working for any personal gain. I'm working for the good of mankind. For world peace. For disarmament. This makes me a dangerous person for those powers who have opposing interests, for those powers working against disarmament, that is to say the military forces, the armament industry, the extreme right-wing nationalists. These enemies of mine have enormous resources. They've done everything to stop me. For a long time they've been waging campaigns against me with millions of dollars. They've pried into my past to find scandals. They've forged false documents to make me appear in an unfavourable light. But they've failed. Instead my followers have snowballed like an avalanche; I've become even more of a threat. Now my enemies are trying to stop me once and for all by killing me. When I use the word enemies, I mean, of course, a small clique out of all my opponents. A small ruthless few who would do anything to get rid of me. They've made three attempts on my life. So far I've survived. But for how long? Sooner or later, they've got to succeed. That is, if I don't take counter-action That was how this idea was born. Maclean and I decided to stage our own attempt on my life. A sensational assassination which would arouse so much attention that it would stop all other attempts.'

The senator again laid his hand on Maclean's shoulder.

'Tell them how you set up this affair,' he said. 'Our best chance is to be completely honest.'

Maclean stared at the ground as if he did not share the senator's opinion that it was an advantage to be honest. Anna wondered what he wanted to do with her and Peter instead. Suddenly she felt frightened.

'If you say so.' Maclean looked up. 'We decided to stage an attempt on the senator. Not any old assassination. Not a single bullet, nor an anonymous bomb. This attempt had to be a first-class sensation which would reverberate through the world press. The final plan of the explosion of a dam here in northern Sweden had many advantages. It was sensational enough. At the same time the actual damage was insignificant. The flood caused here had limited effect. In fact, it ended up in a huge reservoir some kilometres downstream. No risk to human lives.'

'Five dead,' said Peter.

'Let me explain how it was planned,' said Maclean. 'We bought two professional murderers from a European sabotage organization. Both used. Both ready to be discarded. These two were to serve a double purpose. Partly they were to carry out the assassination attempt itself. Partly they were to be scapegoats. Responsible for the operation was Ken Russel, temporarily lent by the CIA, though acting without their direct knowledge. Ken's orders were to take charge of the men in Malmö, instruct them, supervise them on the assignment, and finally liquidate them.'

'We know,' said Peter. 'He meant to leave Steiner's corpse lying by the dam as a clue to who lay behind the assassination. Moll was to be obliterated by the explosion. Ken was going to set out for Norway in Moll's clothing, letting himself be seen by reliable witnesses, and then disappear. Everyone would think that Moll had managed to escape.'

'I can tell Ken Russel told you that,' said Maclean. 'That's only half the picture. The half that Russel knows. You see, he firmly believes that he's carrying out a real assassination which is meant to kill the senator. He also believes that he'll be able to escape after the deed. We haven't planned it that way. The Norwegian contact, who Ken thinks is going to smuggle him out of the country, is really going to turn him over to the police. Ken Russel is going to become the leading defendant in a highly sensational trial.'

'So you've laid a trap for him,' said Anna. She felt upset by Maclean's cold cunning.

'He's completely guilty of the crimes of which he's accused.' Maclean smiled faintly.

'Besides he himself is convinced of it. The court will also find him guilty. The evidence is overwhelming. World opinion will condemn the CIA and the senator's enemies.'

'This trial in Norway will have great historical significance,' said the senator. 'It will be the beginning of a better world. It will be the watershed between the old era with its wars and disturbances and the new era of disarmament and peaceful coexistence. It will open people's eyes.'

'Not to mention that such a trial is fantastic propaganda for you, Senator, just before the presidential election,' said Peter.

'Now let me say something about the presidential election,' said Maclean, turning towards Peter. 'No one in the world is in a better position to work for the cause of world peace than America's president.'

'World peace, you say,' said Peter. 'What great aims you've set for yourselves. It's too bad that you've had to take the lives of so many people to put an end to the killing. You're just the same as all the others. You let the ends justify the means, regardless of the means!'

'You're mistaken,' said the senator. 'No one was supposed to die. Not at the start.'

'Except Steiner and Moll,' said Peter. 'Their function was to blast the dam and then die. You sacrificed them knowingly.'

'Steiner and Moll were both professional murderers with many lives on their consciences,' said Maclean. 'Their organization would have got rid of them in any case. Instead, they died for a good cause.'

'You don't understand the difference between principles and excuses,' said Peter. 'But the senator should. The peace-senator.'

'Maclean promised me that no one innocent would suffer in this operation,' said the senator. 'I believed it. I would never have allowed the sacrificing of a human life in cold blood for any cause, no matter how important. No one deplores more than I do the fact that so many people lost their lives.'

Anna noticed that one of the senator's hands started fidgeting nervously on the buttons of his fishing jacket. Slowly, but nevertheless uncontrolled. Anna interpreted this to indicate that the senator's supreme composure was deserting him.

'You're pulling the wool over your own eyes when you only deplore what's happened and renounce your responsibility for it,' said Peter. 'You deliberately created a violent situation when you accepted the idea of seizing the cottage and its inhabitants and of exploding the dam. The person who creates a violent situation obviously must bear the responsibility of the additional violence which the situation produces.'

The senator stared at the horizon and Anna got the impression that deep within him he agreed with Peter. She thought that Peter was right from beginning to end. She could not understand how a man with the senator's ideals could take part in a plan like like this.

'You obviously don't understand anything!' Maclean threw himself into the debate. 'Don't you understand what we can gain, what a fantastic step forwards we can take? The trial will put the war-hawks in their proper light. Step by step, their conspiracy against the senator will be exposed. It'll focus on the senseless blasting of a dam in a neutral country with innocent people as victims. Press, radio and TV will be there. The whole world will find out about the cruel game our enemies play with human lives. With a nation's welfare!'

'But it's all fraud!' said Peter. 'It isn't your enemies that are behind this senseless explosion. It's you and the senator.'

'Don't call it fraud, call it strategy! We have to defend ourselves somehow. We can't sit still and wait to be annihilated. We must use weapons which achieve our end. The senator has stated clearly what the end involves. The future of mankind!'

'I still don't think that these noble aims justify your actions,' said Peter. 'Quite the opposite. I think your actions desecrate your noble aims.'

'Think whatever you like. The senator asked me to give an account of my planning of the operation, and I've done it. For what it's worth.'

'Yes,' said the senator. 'I have a good reason.' He turned first to Anna and looked her in the eye. Then he turned to Peter. 'I want you both to co-operate with me. That's why I want to be honest with you.'

'I appreciate your honesty,' said Peter. 'Let me be frank as well. I'm not going to play along with your game. In my opinion you're nothing more than an ordinary dictator. You sit in your safe ivory tower of grandiose ideas, press a button and let the bombs drop far away upon innocent people. I ended up right in the middle of your shower of bombs and saw people die. Senator, you're a murderer. And if you think your motive excuses you, I suggest you try explaining it during the trial. Maybe you can convince the court. And world opinion.'

The senator stared at the ground. Anna felt sorry for him. She still saw him as an honest and honourable person, although Peter had exposed his motives as highly suspect. She still wondered how he could have become involved in something like this.

Maclean stuck his hand in under his jacket and pulled out a shining black pistol. He held it in his hand with the muzzle pointing down towards the ground. Anna suddenly realized she was freezing. A cold wind had begun blowing from the mountain chain in the north-east.

'Let me be frank also,' said Maclean to Peter. 'We're a hair's breadth away from the completion of our plan. There's only one detail preventing its complete success. That detail is you!'

'Oh no,' said Anna. 'There's one more detail. Me.'

He looked at her as if she were such a minor detail that she was hardly noticeable. Slowly he raised the pistol so that it pointed at Peter's chest.

'Do you really imagine that we'd let you two get in our way? You're mistaken. We don't need you. We can just as easily use

Haseke and his girlfriend, or whatever she is, as witnesses for the trial. They're sitting out there in the wilderness, just waiting to be brought in to give evidence.'

Suddenly Anna realized that Maclean was pointing the pistol at Peter in order to shoot him. And then her. She wanted to scream but could not make any sound. All the weakness which had affected her earlier during the long hike came back suddenly. A violent nausea rose within her.

'Wait,' came the senator's voice from far away. 'Wait. This won't do!'

'It's perfect. We'll get rid of them here and we'll hide their bodies under some rocks on the slope. Everyone will think they died in the flood. No one will look for them. The warden won't notice anything. He's searching for his dog down along the river. We'll buy him a new dog and he'll be happy.'

'You can't mean this seriously!' The senator took a step towards Maclean. 'You can't tell me that you mean to shoot these two young people in cold blood.'

'Senator, it's the only thing we can do. If we don't get rid of them, all our plans will fall through. We can't allow it to happen.'

'You mean, all your plans!'

The senator stepped in front of Maclean with his chest against the gun muzzle. Anna saw him from the side. His face was pale. His eyes were blazing. Both his hands were clenched hard.

'You know as well as I do that this idea of the faked assassination attempt was yours, not mine,' he continued. 'I went along with it on one condition. That no one was to get hurt. You swore it. Steiner and Moll were to be allowed to escape to Norway and disappear; that was your original plan. Only when things had started did you reveal that you'd made certain changes to the plan. Now Steiner and Moll were to be sacrificed as scapegoats. The new leading role: Ken Russel.'

'I had to give it to you in small doses, just as one gives bitter medicine to a small child,' said Maclean. 'You would never have swallowed the whole dish if I'd given it to you all at once. You're just as soft as all other idealists. That's why you always lose the game. You don't understand that you have to crack an egg to make an omelette. I had to let Steiner and Moll die. To counterbalance your innocence. I had to create a really black-hearted gangster as a symbol for your enemies: Ken Russel. He'll make a tremendous impression during the trial.'

'But I never wanted to have any trial. Little by little, you've forced me into a situation which I didn't want.'

'Don't complain. Look where I've got you. Within the near future you'll run for President of the United States and you can accomplish whatever damned reforms you please!'

'Right now I won't tolerate the execution of two innocent people.'

'You can't back out now. You're in this up to your ears. If you let these two go, it's all over with you. You're finished.'

'You say I can't back out now. That's been your standing argument to get me more and more mixed up in your unscrupulous methods. It's over this minute! No more!'

'What stupidity! You'll end up the accused at the trial!'

'Rather that than be your prisoner for life. Give me the pistol.'

'Move over, Senator. You're in my way.'

'Maclean! The pistol! That's an order!'

'Don't be silly, Senator. You've completely misunderstood the situation. It's a long time since you could give me an order.'

The senator reached out his hand to Maclean to take the pistol from him. Maclean took a step aside, raised his arm and hit the senator in the back of the neck with the pistol. The senator sank slowly to his knees and propped himself against the ground with both hands. Not another sound came from him.

'These damned politicians are all alike,' said Maclean. 'Sooner or later they confuse their image with reality and imagine that they're the ones making the decisions.'

He raised the pistol at Peter.

'Saved by the bell!' Peter pointed at the horizon in the east.

'What do you mean by that?' Maclean didn't take his eyes off him.

'Don't you see the helicopter? It'll be here in two minutes at most. I'm sorry, but you really don't have time both to kill us and hide our corpses.'

'You're bluffing,' said Maclean.

Anna looked up at the horizon. There wasn't a trace of a helicopter. She forced a triumphant smile on to her stiff lips.

'Yes, thank God,' she exclaimed. 'Look! Two of them. What luck!'

She saw Maclean begin to hesitate. Would he dare to shoot without checking whether the helicopters would catch him in the act. On the other hand, would he dare turn around and give Peter the opportunity to leap at him? He solved the problem in a way she had not expected. He took five long steps backwards. That way he was sure of Peter.

Then he turned round.

In the same instant Peter turned round and ran. Anna had never seen anyone run so quickly. Like a hundred-metre sprinter he dashed across the plateau with continual jerks from side to side.

Maclean was taken by surprise. He took a few quick steps forward. Then he stopped and aimed his pistol with arm outstretched. But he did not shoot. It was too late. The distance was too great.

Anna rejoiced within herself. Peter had done exactly the opposite of what Maclean had expected. He had tricked Maclean. He had won the game.

Peter stopped at more than fifty metres' distance when he noticed that Maclean was not following him. He stood completely still with his knees slightly bent so that he could take off again at a moment's notice.

Maclean lowered the pistol. Anna saw that he had realized he had lost. He was too heavy and clumsy to shorten the distance between them. His weapon was not powerful enough to bridge the distance with a shot. In fact, there was nothing he could do. Peter was out of his range.

The senator slowly got up on his feet.

'You're a worthless assistant,' he said. 'It isn't enough that you beat the person you're meant to protect so that everything he's been fighting for is lost. But you also let yourself be tricked by one of the world's oldest tricks.'

He went over to Maclean and took the pistol away from him. Maclean let him without objections. The senator put the safety catch on the pistol and came towards Anna.

'Here you are, miss,' he said. 'You'd better take care of this pistol and hand it over to your young friend. He can have it in his hand when he turns Maclean and me over to the police. It'll look more striking that way.'

The sparkle in the senator's eyes had faded, the wrinkles in his face had deepened, his hair seemed greyer and more aged. He slowly stroked the spot on his neck where Maclean had hit him with the pistol. Anna thought that he looked exactly like what he was: a man who on the way to a great goal, had made a fatal mistake and now realized that he would have to give up everything.

Anna hurried over to Peter with the pistol in her hand. He came to meet her halfway. She gave him the pistol. No hug, no touching, not a smile, not even any thanks. Peter did not let the senator and the security chief, who were standing next to each other like two foiled villains in an old-fashioned melodrama, out of his sight.

'We'll stay here,' said Peter. 'We'll wait for help to come.'

As they stood there silently, next to each other, Anna became intensely aware of the enormous desolation that surrounded them and the tremendous tragedy which they had experienced. She thought about Ken, who even now was on his way to Norway with no idea that he himself was the victim of a plot which would put him in prison for the rest of his active life. Then she thought about the senator. She had admired him and looked up to him. Now she realized that she still admired him and looked up to him. He had tried to save her and Peter although it meant his own ruin. He had attacked Maclean. He had seen his great mistake in going along with the fake assassination. He was prepared to face his punishment.

Anna wondered why the senator's strong moral sense had failed him in this one instance. He must have acted in a panic. Perhaps the explanation was that three assassination attempts had made him terrified that a fourth might succeed.

Anna felt great sympathy for the senator. In order to avoid a fourth attempt he had agreed to a plan which had destroyed him in the end. As effectively as a real assassination. Even more effectively. Now he would not even become a martyr for the cause of world peace. Instead he would be exposed as a fraud in a public trial. His enemies could not have planned it better themselves.

Maybe that was exactly what they'd done!

For the first time Anna felt that she had a general view over all the events. Earlier, they'd been hurled at her so quickly that she had barely been able to duck one before the next one was on the way. Peter had managed much better than she, after he had overcome his fear in the struggle with Ken down by the river. He had been able to survey events, analyse them and influence them. In the end, he had even become a man of action.

For the first time she saw a pattern. But it was not the one Peter saw. It was as if she had taken a step backwards to get a new perspective and now saw a new pattern emerge in the same picture. She was far from sure about her idea, but this unsuccessful assassination, which in the end succeeded in destroying the senator . . . was it not planned by his enemies?

'Peter,' she said. 'Listen! Listen carefully! Suppose the three previous assassination attempts were just warning shots to lure the senator into a fourth attempt. A different attempt. Not an attempt which aimed to take his life—that would make him a martyr and arouse people's anger against the conspirators. No, an attempt which aimed for a much more refined way of getting rid of him. An attempt which was a trap. In that case the attempt has succeeded. The trap's been sprung. The senator has been lured into destroying himself. The trial in Norway will be an enormous catastrophe. Not only for the senator, but also for his cause: disarmament and world peace. His enemies will triumph. Greatly.'

'I've been thinking the same thing,' said Peter. 'It's possible you're right. Maclean could secretly be working for the senator's enemies. Why didn't he shoot me when I was running? Or does Ken play a larger part than we thought? Maybe he never meant to kill us up there in the mountains. What if he only wanted to make us think that. Perhaps he isn't planning to make that contact in Norway, but is going to disappear on his own and let the senator stand alone in the dock as the accused. Or else everything's been arranged in a third way; but we'll never know.'

'But what should we do?'

'I don't know.'

'We have to decide something. The helicopters and the police will soon be here. Think how we've suffered, even risked our lives, all to save the senator. Are we now going to torpedo him ourselves? It would be terrible!'

'Let's try to sort this out. We've two alternatives to choose from. Either tell as much of the truth as we know and let the catastrophe destroy the senator. Or else, we keep the truth a secret and let the senator win the game. In the first case, we become tools of the warmongers in stopping the foremost champion for disarmament and peace. In the second we condone a man benefiting from a serious crime which caused great destruction and death.'

Peter paused and looked at Anna.

'Whichever choice we make,' he said, 'it's the wrong one.'

'That depends,' said Anna. 'You men have an incredible talent for thinking of logical alternatives and rigid either-ors. But there's another way of thinking, a more feminine way, the way in which I, at any rate, think. We can really solve the problem that way.'

Peter looked at her doubtfully.

'The senator is here in great secrecy. No one has any idea of his presence except those involved. Suppose that his presence remains a secret. In that case neither of your two alternatives occurs. The senator is neither destroyed, nor victorious.'

A smile lit in Peter's eyes and spread slowly to his lips.

'You're a genius, Anna,' he said.

Then he looked across the endless plateau towards the west and continued: 'But Haseke and Sabine? When they're eventually rescued, naturally they'll tell what happened to them.'

'Only you and I know the truth, that is, that the senator himself is involved in the assassination attempt. The others don't know anything about that, not Haseke, not Sabine, not the warden of this place. In their eyes the senator is a hero, who barely escaped being killed. It'll be easy for the senator to get them to co-operate. And it'll be just as easy for him to get those who are indirectly involved on his side. He won't find it hard to hush up the whole story. The Swedish authorities will do everything to help him. Just think what a diplomatic scandal he's saving them from that way.'

'But how can all the deaths be explained? The housekeeper, Grahn, the major, Steiner and Moll?'

'They can be accounted for by the flood. If the case is treated with discretion by the authorities, no one will suspect anything other than that the flood occurred because of an unfortunate bursting of the dam. If Steiner's corpse, as originally planned, had remained by the dam, it would have been a problem. But Ken can't have managed to carry him up there after chasing us. Instead, he probably left Steiner's identification papers there. They can easily be removed. The senator and Maclean can take care of that. They simply can't afford to fail. If they did, you and I would tell the whole truth and they'd be destroyed by the catastrophe.'

'And Ken?'

'Ken won't reach Norway for at least another twenty-four hours. Maclean has plenty of time to remove the trap and let the contact help Ken get out of the country.'

'In other words he'll get away.'

'If we're going to adopt a moralistic attitude to this, then the murders of the housekeeper, Grahn and the major have been punished: Steiner and Moll are dead. I think that's enough. I don't mind if Ken gets away as long as I don't have to see him again.'

'You liked him.'

'I liked him until he started trying to kill me. But now we have to settle this with senator. There's very little time. The helicopters will be here any minute now. You take care of it. I'll wait here.'

At first Peter seemed about to protest, then he nodded, turned on his heel and walked over to the senator and Maclean. She looked around for something to lean her back against, found a suitable stone, and sat down with difficulty.

When Peter reached the two men he turned to the senator. The distance was too great for Anna to understand what they were saying. That suited her perfectly. She did not have enough energy to participate any more. She was too tired.

But she no longer felt the exhaustion as a nuisance. She accepted the muscle pains in her legs like an older person; it was beginning to be a habit. She felt as if she had done her bit and was now enjoying her well deserved rest.

She had done even more than her bit. She had solved a problem insoluble by the others and had arranged a decent end to the affair. She wondered how right she was in believing that her solution derived from a typically female way of thinking, which could open all the locked positions in the man's world.

The three men on the edge of the plateau were still talking. Anna was sure that the senator would accept. She was happy for his sake. She understood now how he could have landed himself in a situation which contradicted his principles. She thought that this must be the condition of many politicians: bound hand and foot, they had to play a game directed by others, which they despised, and yet for which they had to take the responsibility.

She noticed that the birds with their fluttering and cries were gone. White clouds drifted over Lektivagge Mountain concealing the crime at the Paktas dam with their beauty.

Suddenly she noticed the senator stretch out his hand and shake hands with Peter as if to confirm an agreement. Maclean did the same. Peter offered him the pistol. He took it and it disappeared under his jacket. Everything seemed to go according to plan.

Peter started walking towards her. She could see by his face that her suggestion had been accepted.

'They're grateful,' he said. 'The senator from his heart and Maclean from commonsense. Petterson, the warden, won't be a problem. Maclean will offer him a handsome pension which he'll get every year that the senator's presence here remains a secret. Haseke can certainly be persuaded as well. The director of a travel company would certainly do a favour for an influential senator and possible future president, if he can count on being repaid a hundred times over—and Ken will be helped to a safe place.'

'And you and I?'

'We'll tell how we set out on an expedition along the river and in that way were lucky enough to avoid the flood, which obviously killed the others. Of course, we don't know how it happened. The dam must have burst by accident.'

'And the rest?' Anna closed her eyes and once again the distressing events whirled past in her mind. She opened her eyes and saw the cold blue indifference of the sky. Then she looked at Peter and a warm wave surged through her.

'Yes,' she said.

Then she gave him her hand.

'The rest is silence.'